A NATIONAL SURVEY ...

He gradually built up a picture of a people being systematically and thoroughly enslaved, a picture of a nation as helpless as a man completely paralyzed, its defenses destroyed, its communications entirely in the hands of the invaders.

Everywhere he found boiling resentment, a fierce willingness to fight against the tyranny, but it was undirected, uncoordinated, and, in any modern sense, unarmed. Sporadic rebellion was as futile as the scurrying of ants whose hill has been violated. PanAsians could be killed, yes, and there were men willing to shoot on sight, even in the face of the certainty of their own deaths. But their hands were bound by the greater certainty of brutal multiple retaliation against their own kind. As with the Jews in Germany before the final blackout in Europe, bravery was not enough, for one act of violence against the tyrants would be paid for by other men, women, and children at unspeakable compound interest.

ROBERT A. HEINLEIN

SIXTH COLUMN

science fiction

Distributed in Canada by PaperJacks Ltd., a Licensee
of the trademarks of Simon & Schuster, Inc.

SIXTH COLUMN

A Baen Book

In Canada distributed by PaperJacks Ltd.,
330 Steelcase Road, Markham, Ontario

First Baen printing, January 1988

ISBN: 0-671-65374-1

Cover art by John Melo

Printed in Canada

Distributed by
SIMON & SCHUSTER
1230 Avenue of the Americas
New York, N.Y. 10020

For John S. Arwine

CHAPTER ONE

"WHAT THE HELL GOES ON HERE?" WHITEY ARD-more demanded.

They ignored his remark as they had ignored his arrival. The man at the television receiver said, "Shut up. We're listening," and turned up the volume. The announcer's voice blared out: "—Washington destroyed completely before the government could escape. With Manhattan in ruins, that leaves no—"

There was a click as the receiver was turned off. "That's that," said the man near it. "The United States is washed up." Then he added, "Anybody got a cigarette?"

Getting no answer, he pushed his way out of the small circle gathered around the receiver and felt through the pockets of a dozen figures collapsed by a table. It was not too easy, as rigor mortis had set in, but he finally located a half-empty pack, from which he removed a cigarette and lighted it.

"Somebody answer me!" commanded Ardmore. "What's happened here?"

The man with the cigarette looked him over for the first time. "Who are you?"

"Ardmore, major, intelligence. Who are *you*?"

"Calhoun, colonel in research."

"Very well, Colonel—I have an urgent message for your commanding officer. Will you please have someone tell him that I am here and see to it that I am taken to him?" He spoke with poorly controlled exasperation.

Calhoun shook his head. "Can't do it. He's dead." He seemed to derive some sort of twisted pleasure from the announcement.

"Huh?"

"That's right—dead. They're all dead, all the rest. You see before you, my dear Major, all that are left of the personnel of the Citadel—perhaps I should say of the emergency research laboratory, department of defense, this being in the nature of an official report." He smiled with half his face, while his eye took in the handful of living men in the room.

Ardmore took a moment to comprehend the statement, then inquired, "The PanAsians?"

"No. No, not the PanAsians. So far as I know, the enemy does not suspect the existence of the Citadel. No, we did it ourselves—an experiment that worked too well. Dr. Ledbetter was engaged in research in an attempt to discover a means of—"

"Never mind that, Colonel. Whom does command revert to? I've got to carry out my orers."

"Command? Military command? Good Lord, man, we haven't had time to think about that—yet. Wait a moment." His eye roved around the room, counting noses. "Hm-m-m—I'm senior to everyone here—and they are all here. I suppose that makes me commanding officer."

"No line officers present?"

"No. All special commissions. That leaves me it. Go ahead with your report."

Ardmore looked about at the faces of the half a dozen men in the room. They were following the conversation with apathetic interest. Ardmore worried to himself before replying over how to phrase the message. The situation had changed; perhaps he should not deliver it at all—

"I was ordered," he said, picking his words, "to inform your general that he was released from superior command. He was to operate independently and prosecute the war against the invader according to his own judgment. You see," he went on, "when I left Washington twelve hours ago we knew they had us. This concentration of brain power in the Citadel was about the only remaining possible military asset."

Calhoun nodded. "I see. A defunct government sends orders to a defunct laboratory. Zero plus zero equals zero. It's all very funny if one only knew when to laugh."

"Colonel!"

"Yes?"

"They are your orders now. What do you propose to do with them?"

"Do with them? What the hell is there to do? Six men against four hundred million. I suppose," he

3

added "to make everything nice and tidy for the military mind I should write out a discharge from the United States army for everybody left and kiss 'em good-by. I don't know where that leaves me—hara-kiri, perhaps. Maybe you don't get it. This is all the United States there is left. And it's left because the PanAsians haven't found it."

Ardmore wet his lips. "Apparently I did not clearly convey the order. The order was to take charge, *and prosecute the war!*"

"With what?"

He measured Calhoun before answering. "It is not actually your responsibility. Under the changed situation, in accordance with the articles of war, as senior line officer present I am assuming command of this detachment of the United States army!"

It hung in the balance for twenty heartbeats. At last Calhoun stood up and attempted to square his stooped shoulders. "You are perfectly correct, sir. What are your orders?"

"What are your orders?" he asked himself. Think fast, Ardmore, you big lunk, you've shot off your face—now where are you? Calhoun was right when he asked "With what?"—yet he could not stand still and see the remnant of military organization fall to pieces.

You've got to tell 'em something, and it's got to be good; at least good enough to hold 'em until you think of something better. Stall, brother, stall! "I think we had best examine the new situation here, first. Colonel, will you oblige me by having the remaining

4

personnel gather around—say around that big table? That will be convenient."

"Certainly, sir." The others, having heard the order, moved toward the table. "Graham! And you— what's your name? Thomas, isn't it? You two remove Captain MacAllister's body to some other place. Put him in the corridor for now."

The commotion of getting one of the ubiquitous corpses out of the way and getting the living settled around a table broke the air of unreality and brought things into focus. Ardmore felt more self-confidence when he turned again to Calhoun. "You had better introduce me to those here present. I want to know what they do and something about them, as well as their names."

It was a corporal's guard, a forlorn remnant. He had expected to find, hidden here safely and secretly away under an unmarked spot in the Rocky Mountains, the most magnificent aggregation of research brains ever gathered together for one purpose. Even in the face of complete military disaster to the regular forces of the United States, there remained a reasonable outside chance that two hundred-odd keen scientific brains, secreted in a hide-away whose very existence was unsuspected by the enemy and equipped with every modern facility for research, might conceivably perfect and operate some weapon that would eventually drive out the PanAsians.

For that purpose he had been sent to tell the commanding general that he was on his own, no longer responsible to higher authority. But what could half a dozen men do in any case?

For it was a scant half a dozen. There was Dr.

Lowell Calhoun, mathematician, jerked out of university life by the exigencies of war and called a colonel. There was Dr. Randall Brooks, biologist and bio-chemist, with a special commission of major. Ardmore liked his looks; he was quiet and mild, but gave the impression of an untroubled strength of character superior to that of a more extroverted man—he would do, and his advice would be useful.

Ardmore mentally dubbed Robert Wilkie a "punk kid." He was young and looked younger, having an overgrown collie-dog clumsiness, and hair that would not stay in place. His field, it developed, was radiation, and the attendant branches of physics too esoteric for a layman to understand. Ardmore had not the slighest way of judging whether or not he was any good in his specialty. He might be a genius, but his appearance did not encourage the idea.

No other scientist remained. There were three enlisted men: Herman Scheer, technical sergeant. He had been a mechanic, a die maker, a tool maker. When the army picked him up he had been making precision instruments for the laboratories of the Edison Trust. His brown, square hands and lean fingers backed up his account of himself. His lined, set face and heavy jaw muscles made Ardmore judge him to be a good man to have at his back in a tight place. He would do.

There remained Edward Graham, private first-class, specialist rating officers' cook. Total war had turned him from his profession as an artist and interior decorator to his one other talent, cooking. Ardmore was unable to see how he could fit into the job, except, of course, that somebody had to cook.

The last man was Graham's helper, Jeff Thomas, private—background: none. "He wandered in here one day," explained Calhoun. "We had to enlist him and keep him here to protect the secret of the place."

Acquainting Ardmore with the individuals of his "command" had used up several minutes during which he had thought furiously with half his mind about what he should say next. He knew what he had to accomplish, some sort of a shot in the arm that would restore the morale of this badly demoralized group, some of the old hokum that men live by. He believed in hokum, being a publicity man by trade and an army man only by necessity. That brought to mind another worry—should he let them know that he was no more a professional than they, even though he happened to hold a line commission? No, that would not be very bright; they needed just now to regard him with the faith that the layman usually holds for the professional.

Thomas was the end of the list: Calhoun had stopped talking. Here's your chance, son, better not muff it!

Then he had it—fortunately it would take only a short build-up. "It will be necessary for us to continue our task assignment independently for an indefinite period. I want to remind you that we derive our obligations not from our superior officers who were killed in Washington, but from the people of the United States, through their Constitution. That Constitution is neither captured nor destroyed—it cannot, for it is not a piece of paper, but the joint contract of the American people. Only the American people can release us from it."

Was he right? He was no lawyer, and he didn't know—but he did know that they needed to believe it. He turned to Calhoun. "Colonel Calhoun, will you now swear me in as commanding officer of this detachment of the United States army?" Then he added, as an apparent afterthought, "I think it would be well for us all to renew our oaths at the same time."

It was a chanted chorus that echoed through the nearly empty room. " 'I do solemnly swear—to carry out the duties of my office—and to uphold and defend the Constitution of the United States—against all of its enemies, domestic and foreign!'

"So help me God."

" *'So help me God!'* "

Ardmore was surprised to discover that the show he had staged brought tears to his own cheeks. Then he noticed them in Calhoun's eyes. Maybe there was more to it than he had thought.

"Colonel Calhoun, you, of course, become director of research. You are second in command, but I will carry out the duties of executive officer myself in order to leave you free to pursue your scientific inquiries. Major Brooks and Captain Wilkie are assigned to you. Scheer!"

"Yes, sir!"

"You work for Colonel Calhoun. If he does not need all of your service, I will assign additional duties later. Graham!"

"Yes, sir."

"You will continue your present duties. You are also mess sergeant, mess officer, supply officer—in fact, you are the whole commissary department. Bring me a report later today estimating the number of rations available and the condition of perishables. Thomas works for you, but is subject to call by any member of the scientific staff any time they want him. That may delay meals, but it can't be helped."

"Yes, sir."

"You and I and Thomas will perform all duties among us that do not directly apply to research, and will assist the scientists in any way and at any time that they need us. That specifically includes myself, Colonel," he emphasized, turning to Calhoun, "if another pair of untrained hands is useful at any point, you are directed to call on me."

"Very well, Major."

"Graham, you and Thomas will have to clear out the bodies around the place before they get too high—say by tomorrow night. Put them in an unused room and hermetically seal it. Scheer will show you how." He glanced at his wrist. "Two o'clock. When did you have lunch?"

"There . . . uh . . . was none today."

"Very well. Graham, serve coffee and sandwiches here in twenty minutes."

"Very good, sir. Come along, Jeff."

"Coming."

As they left, Ardmore turned back to Calhoun. "In the meantime, Colonel, let's go to the laboratory where the catastrophe originated. I *still* want to find out what happened here!"

The other two scientists and Scheer hesitated; he picked them up with a nod, and the little party filed out.

*   *   *

"You say nothing in particular happened, no explosion, no gas—yet they died?" They were standing around Dr. Ledbetter's last set-up. The martyred scientist's body still lay where it had fallen, a helpless, disorganized heap. Ardmore took his eyes from it and tried to make out the meaning of the set-up apparatus. It looked simple, but called no familiar picture to mind.

"No, nothing but a little blue flame that persisted momentarily. Ledbetter had just closed this switch." Calhoun pointed to it without touching it. It was open now, a self-opening, spring-loaded type. "I felt suddenly dizzy. When my head cleared, I saw that Ledbetter had fallen and went to him, but there was nothing that I could do for him. He was dead—without a mark on him."

"It knocked me out," offered Wilkie. "I might not have made it if Scheer hadn't given me artificial respiration."

"You were here?" Ardmore asked.

"No, I was in the radiation laboratory over at the other end of the plant. It killed my chief."

Ardmore frowned and pulled a chair out from the wall. As he started to sit down there was a scurrying sound, a small gray shape flashed across the floor and out the open door. A rat, he thought, and dismissed the matter. But Dr. Brooks stared at it in amazement, and ran out the door himself, calling out behind him: "Wait a minute—right back!"

"I wonder what's gotten into him?" Ardmore inquired of no one in particular. The thought flashed through his mind that the strain of events had finally been too much for the mild little biologist.

They had less than a minute to wait in order to find out. Brooks returned as precipitately as he had left. The exertion caused him to pant and interfered with articulation. "Major Ardmore! Dr. Calhoun! Gentlemen!" He paused and caught his breath. "My white mice are alive!"

"Huh? What of it?"

"Don't you see? It's an important datum, perhaps a crucially important datum. None of the animals in the biological laboratory was hurt! Don't you see?"

"Yes, but— Oh! Perhaps I do—the rat was alive and your mice weren't killed, yet men were killed all around them."

"Of course! Of course!" Brooks beamed at Ardmore.

"Hm-m-m. An action that kills a couple of hundred men through rock walls and metal, with no fuss and no excitement, yet passes by mice and the like. I've never before heard of anything that would kill a man but not a mouse." He nodded toward the apparatus. "It looks as if we had big medicine in that little gadget, Calhoun."

"So it does," Calhoun agreed, "if we can learn to control it."

"Any doubt in your mind?"

"Well—we don't know why it killed, and we don't know why it spared six of us, and we don't know why it doesn't harm animals."

"So— Well, that seems to be the problem." He stared again at the simple-appearing enigma. "Doctor, I don't like to interfere with your work right from scratch, but I would rather you did not close that switch without notifying me in advance." His gaze dropped to Ledbetter's still figure and hurriedly shifted.

Over the coffee and sandwiches he pried further into the situation. "Then no one really knows what Ledbetter was up to?"

"You could put it that way," agreed Calhoun. "I helped him with the mathematical considerations, but he was a genius and somewhat impatient with lesser minds. If Einstein were alive, they might have talked as equals, but with the rest of us he discussed only the portions he wanted assistance on, or details he wished to turn over to assistants."

"Then you don't know what he was getting at?"

"Well, yes and no. Are you familiar with general field theory?"

"Criminy, no!"

"Well—that makes it rather hard to talk, Major Ardmore. Dr. Ledbetter was investigating the theoretically possible additional spectra—"

"Additional spectra?"

"Yes. You see, most of the progress in physics in the last century and a half has been in dealing with the electromagnetic spectrum, light, radio, X-ray—"

"Yes, yes, I know that, but how about these additional spectra?"

"That's what I am trying to tell you," answered Calhoun with a slight note of annoyance. "General field theory predicts the possibility of at least three more entire spectra. You see, there are three types of energy fields known to exist in space: electric, magnetic, and gravitic or gravitational. Light, X-rays, all such radiations, are part of the electromagnetic spectrum. Theory indicates the possibility of analogous spectra between magnetic and gravitic, between electric and gravitic, and finally, a three-phase type between electric-magnetic-gravitic fields. Each type would constitute a complete new spectrum, a total of three new fields of learning.

"If there are such, they would presumably have properties quite as remarkable as the electromagnetic spectrum and quite different. But we have no instruments with which to detect such spectra, nor do we even know that such spectra exist."

"You know," commented Ardmore, frowning a little, "I'm just a layman in these matters and don't wish to set my opinion up against yours, but this seems like a search for the little man who wasn't there. I had supposed that this laboratory was engaged in the single purpose of finding a military weapon to combat the vortex beams and A-bomb rockets of the PanAsians. I am a bit surprised to find the man whom you seem to regard as having been your ace researcher engaged in an attempt to discover things that he was not sure existed and whose properties were totally unknown. It doesn't seem reasonable."

Calhoun did not answer; he simply looked supercilious and smiled irritatingly. Ardmore felt put in the wrong and was conscious of a warm flush spreading up toward his face. "Yes, yes," he said hastily, "I know I'm wrong—whatever it was that Ledbetter found, it killed a couple of hundred men. Therefore it is a potential military weapon—but wasn't he just mugging around in the dark?"

"Not entirely," Calhoun replied, with a words-of-one-syllable air. "The very theoretical considerations that predict additional spectra allow of some reasonable probability as to the general nature of their properties. I know that Ledbetter had originally been engaged in a search for a means of setting up tractor and pressor beams—that would be in the magneto-gravitic spectrum—but the last couple of weeks he appeared to be in a condition of intense excitement and radically changed the direction of his experimentation. He was close-mouthed; I got no more than a few hints from the transformations and developments which he had me perform for him. However"—Calhoun drew a bulky loose-leaf notebook from an inner pocket—"he kept complete notes of his experiments. We should be able to follow his work and perhaps infer his hypotheses."

Young Wilkie, who was seated beside Calhoun, bent toward him. "Where did you find these, doctor?" he asked excitedly.

"On a bench in his laboratory. If you had looked you would have seen them."

Wilkie ignored the thrust; he was already eating up the symbols set down in the opened book. "But that is a radiation formula—"

"Of course it is—d'you think I'm a fool?"

"But it's all wrong!"

"It may be from your standpoint; you may be sure that it was not to Dr. Ledbetter."

They branched off into argument that was totally meaningless to Ardmore; after some minutes he took advantage of a pause to say, "Gentlemen! Gentlemen! Just a moment. I can see that I am simply keeping you from your work; I've learned all that I can just now. As I understand it, your immediate task is to catch up with Dr. Ledbetter and to discover what it is that his apparatus does—*without* killing yourselves in the process. Is that right?"

"I would say that is a fair statement," Calhoun agreed cautiously.

"Very well, then—carry on, and keep me advised at your convenience." He got up; the others followed his example. "Oh—just one more thing."

"Yes?"

"I happened to think of something else. I don't know whether it is important or not, but it came to mind because of the importance that Dr. Brooks attached to the matter of the rats and mice." He ticked points off on his fingers. "Many men were killed; Dr. Wilkie was knocked out and very nearly died; Dr. Calhoun experienced only a momentary discomfort; the rest of those who lived apparently didn't suffer any effects of any sort—weren't aware that anything had happened except that their companions mysteriously died. Now, isn't that data of some sort?" He awaited a reply anxiously, being subconsciously afraid that the scientists would consider his remarks silly, or obvious.

Calhoun started to reply, but Dr. Brooks cut in ahead of him. "Of course, it is! Now why didn't I think of that? Dear me, I must be confused today. That establishes a gradient, an ordered relationship in the effect of the unknown action." He stopped and thought, then went on almost at once. "I really must have your permission, Major, to examine the cadavers of our late colleagues, then by examining for differences between them and those alive, especially those hard hit by the unknown action—" He broke off short and eyed Wilkie speculatively.

"No, you don't!" protested Wilkie. "You won't make a guinea pig out of me. Not while I know it!" Ardmore was unable to tell whether the man's apprehension was real or facetious. He cut it short.

"The details will have to be up to you gentlemen. But remember—no chances to your lives without notifying me."

"You hear that, Brooksie?" Wilkie persisted.

Ardmore went to bed that night from sheer sense of duty, not because he felt ready to sleep. His immediate job was accomplished; he had picked up the pieces of the organization known as the Citadel and had thrown it together into some sort of a going concern—whether or not it was going any place he was too tired to judge, but at least it was going. He had given them a pattern to live by, and, by assuming leadership and responsibility, had enabled them to unload their basic worries on him and thereby acquire some measure of emotional security. That should keep them from going crazy in a world which had gone crazy.

What would it be like, this crazy new world—a world in which the superiority of western culture was not a casualty accepted 'Of course,' a world in which the Stars and Stripes did not fly, along with the pigeons, over every public building?

Which brought to mind a new worry: if he was to maintain any pretense of military purpose, he would have to have some sort of a service of information.

He had been too busy in getting them all back to work to think about it, but he would have to think about it—tomorrow, he told himself, then continued to worry about it.

An intelligence service was as important as a new secret weapon—more important; no matter how fantastic and powerful a weapon might be developed from Dr. Ledbetter's researches, it would be no help until they knew just where and how to use it against the enemy's weak points. A ridiculously inadequate military intelligence had been the prime characteristic of the United States as a power all through its history. The most powerful nation the globe had ever seen—but it had stumbled into wars like a blind giant. Take this present mess: the atom bombs of PanAsia weren't any more powerful than our own— but we had been caught flat-footed and had never gotten to use a one.

We had had how many stock-piled? A thousand, he had heard. Ardmore didn't know, but certainly the PanAsians had known, just how many, just where they were. Military intelligence had won the war for them, not secret weapons. Not that the secret weapons of the PanAsians were anything to sneer at— particularly when it was all too evident that they really were "secret." Our own so-called intelligence services had fallen down on the job.

O.K., Whitey Ardmore, it's all yours now! You can build any sort of an intelligence service your heart desires—using three near-sighted laboratory scientists, an elderly master sergeant, two kitchen privates, and the bright boy in person. So you are good at criticizing—"If you're so smart, why ain't you rich?"

He got up, wished passionately for just one dose of barbiturate to give him a night's sleep, drank a glass of hot water instead, and went back to bed.

Suppose they did dig up a really powerful and new weapon? That gadget of Ledbetter's certainly looked good, if they could learn to handle it—but what then? One man couldn't run a battle cruiser—he couldn't even get it off the ground—and six men couldn't whip an empire, not even with seven-league boots and a death ray. What was that old crack of Archimedes? "If I had a lever long enough and a fulcrum on which to rest it, I could move the Earth." How about the fulcrum? No weapon was a weapon without an army to use it.

He dropped into a light sleep and dreamed that he was flopping around on the end of the longest lever conceivable, a useless lever, for it rested on nothing. Part of the time he was Archimedes, and part of the time Archimedes stood beside him, jeering and leering at him with a strongly Asiatic countenance.

CHAPTER TWO

ARDMORE WAS TOO BUSY FOR THE NEXT COUPLE OF weeks to worry much about anything but the job at hand. The underlying postulate of their existence pattern—that they were, *in fact*, a military organization which must some day render an accounting to civil authority—required that he should comply with, or closely simulate compliance with, the regulations concerning paperwork, reports, records, pay accounts, inventories, and the like. In his heart he felt it to be waste motion, senseless, yet as a publicity man, he was enough of a jackleg psychologist to realize intuitively that man is a creature that lives by symbols. At the moment these symbols of government were all important.

So he dug into the regulation manual of the deceased paymaster and carefully closed out the accounts of the dead, noting in each case the amounts due each man's dependents "in lawful money of the United States," even while wondering despondently if that neat phrase would ever mean anything again. But he did it, and he assigned minor administrative jobs to each of the others in order that they might realize indirectly that the customs were being maintained.

It was too much clerical work for one man to keep up. He discovered that Jeff Thomas, the cook's helper, could use a typewriter with facility and had a fair head for figures. He impressed him into the job. It threw more work on Graham, who complained, but that was good for him, he thought—a dog needs fleas. He wanted every member of his command to go to bed tired every night.

Thomas served another purpose. Ardmore's highstrung disposition required someone to talk to. Thomas turned out to be intelligent and passively sympathetic, and he found himself speaking with more and more freedom to the man. It was not in character for the commanding officer to confide in a private, but he felt instinctively that Thomas would not abuse his trust—and he needed nervous release.

Calhoun brought up the matter which forced Ardmore to drop his preoccupation with routine and turn his attention to more difficult matters. Calhoun had called to ask permission to activate Ledbetter's apparatus, as modified to suit their current hypotheses, but he added another and embarrassing question.

"Major Ardmore, can you give me some idea as to how you intend to make use of the 'Ledbetter effect'?"

Ardmore did not know; he answered with another question. "Are you near enough to results to make that question urgent? If so, can you give me some idea of what you have discovered so far?"

"That will be difficult," Calhoun replied in an academic and faintly patronizing manner, "since I am constrained not to speak in the mathematical language which, of necessity, is the only way of expressing such things—"

"Now, Colonel, please," Ardmore broke in, irritated more than he would admit to himself and inhibited by the presence of Private Thomas, "you can kill a man with it or you can't and you can control whom you kill or you can't."

"That's an oversimplification," Calhoun argued. "However, we think that the new set-up will be directional in its effect. Dr. Brook's investigations caused him to hypothecate an asymmetrical relationship between the action and organic life it is applied to, such that an inherent characteristic of the life form determines the effect of the action as well as the inherent characteristics of the action itself. That is to say, the effect is a function of the total factors of the process, including the life form involved, as well as the original action—"

"Easy, easy, Colonel. What does that mean as a weapon?"

"It means that you could turn it on two men and decide which one it is to kill—with proper controls," Calhoun answered testily. "At least, we think so. Wilkie has volunteered to act as a control on it, with mice as the object."

Ardmore granted permission for the experiment to take place, subject to precautions and restrictions.

When Calhoun had gone, his mind returned at once to the problem of what he was going to do with the weapon—if any. And that required data that he did not have. Damn it!—he had to have a service of information; he *had* to know what was going on outside.

The scientists were out, of course. And Scheer, for the scientific staff needed his skill. Graham? No, Graham was a good cook, but nervous and irritable, emotionally not stable, the very last man to pick for a piece of dangerous espionage. It left only himself. He was trained for such things; he would have to go.

"But you can't do that, sir," Thomas reminded him.

"Huh? What's that?" He had been unconsciously expressing his thoughts aloud, a habit he had gotten into when he was alone, or with Thomas only. The man's manner encouraged using him for a sounding board.

"You can't leave your command, sir. Not only is it against regulations, but, if you will let me express an opinion, everything you have done so far will fall to pieces."

"Why should it? I'll be back in a few days."

"Well, sir, maybe it would hold together for a few days—though I'm not sure of that. Who would be in charge in your absence?"

"Colonel Calhoun—of course."

"Of course." Thomas expressed by raised eyebrows and ready agreement an opinion which military courtesy did not permit him to say aloud. Ardmore knew that Thomas was right. Outside of his specialty, Calhoun was a bad-tempered, supercilious, conceited old fool, in Ardmore's opinion. Ardmore had had to intercede already to patch up trouble which Calhoun's arrogance had caused. Scheer worked for Calhoun only because Ardmore had talked with him, calmed him down, and worked on his strong sense of duty.

The situation reminded him of the time when he had worked as press agent for a famous and successful female evangelist. He had signed on as director of public relations, but he had spent two-thirds of his time straightening out the messes caused by the vicious temper of the holy harridan.

"But you have no way of being sure that you will be back in a few days," Thomas persisted. "This is a very dangerous assignment; if you get killed on it, there is no one here who can take over your job."

"Oh, now, that's not true, Thomas. No man is irreplaceable."

"This is no time for false modesty, sir. That may be true in general, but you know that it is not true in this case. There is a strictly limited number to draw from, and you are the only one from whom all of us will take direction. In particular, you are the only one from whom Dr. Calhoun will take direction. That is because you know how to handle him. None of the others would be able to, nor would he be able to handle them."

"That's a pretty strong statement, Thomas."

Thomas said nothing. At length Ardmore went on. "All right, all right—suppose you are right. I've got to have military information. How am I going to get it if I don't go myself?"

Thomas was a little slow in replying. Finally, he said quietly, "I could try it."

"You?" Ardmore looked him over and wondered why he had not considered Thomas. Perhaps because there was nothing about the man to suggest his potential ability to handle such a job—that, combined with the fact that he was a private, and one did not assign privates to jobs requiring dangerous independent action. Yet perhaps—

"Have you ever done any work of that sort?"

"No, but my experience may be specially adapted in a way to such work."

"Oh, yes! Scheer told me something about you. You were a tramp, weren't you, before the army caught up with you?"

"Not a tramp," Thomas corrected gently, "a hobo."

"Sorry—what's the distinction?"

"A tramp is a bum, a parasite, a man that won't work. A hobo is an itinerant laborer who prefers casual freedom to security. He works for his living, but he won't be tied down to one environment."

"Oh, I see. Hm-m-m—yes, and I begin to see why you might be especially well adapted to an intelligence job. I suppose it must require a good deal of adaptibility and resourcefulness to stay alive as a hobo. But wait a minute, Thomas—I guess I've more or less taken you for granted; I need to know a great deal more about you, if you are to be entrusted with this job. You know, you don't *act* like a hobo."

"How does a hobo act?"

"Eh? Oh, well, skip it. But tell me something about your background. How did you happen to take up hoboing?"

Ardmore realized that he had, for the first time, pierced the man's natural reticence. Thomas fumbled for an answer, finally replying, "I suppose it was that I did not like being a lawyer."

"What?"

"Yes. You see, it was like this: I went from the law into social administration. In the course of my work I got an idea that I wanted to write a thesis on migratory labor and decided that in order to understand the subject I would have to experience the conditions under which such people lived."

"I see. And it was while you were doing your laboratory work, as it were, that the army snagged you."

"Oh, no," Thomas corrected him. "I've been on the road more than ten years. I never went back. You see, I found I liked being a hobo."

The details were rapidly arranged. Thomas wanted nothing in the way of equipment but the clothes he had been wearing when he had stumbled into the Citadel. Ardmore had suggested a bedding roll, but Thomas would have none of it. "It would not be in character," he explained. "I was never a bindlestiff. Bindlestiffs are dirty, and a self-respecting hobo doesn't associate with them. All I want is a good meal in my belly and a small amount of money on my person."

Ardmore's instructions to him were very general. "Almost anything you hear or see will be data for me," he told him. "Cover as much territory as you can, and try to be back here within a week. If you are gone much longer than that, I will assume that you are dead or imprisoned, and will have to try some other plan.

"Keep your eyes open for some means by which we can establish a permanent service of information. I can't suggest what it is you are to look for in that connection, but keep it in mind. Now as to details: anything and everything about the PanAsians, how they are armed, how they police occupied territory, where they have set up headquarters, particularly their continental headquarters, and, if you can make any sort of estimate, how many of them there are and how they're distributed. That would keep you busy for a year, at least; just the same, be back in a week."

Ardmore showed Thomas how to operate one of the outer doors of the Citadel; two bars of "Yankee Doodle," breaking off short, and a door appeared in what seemed to be a wall of country rock—simple, and yet foreign to the Asiatic mind. Then he shook hands with him and wished him good luck.

Ardmore found that Thomas had still one more surprise for him; when he shook hands, he did so with the grip of the Dekes, Ardmore's own fraternity! Ardmore stood staring at the closed portal, busy arranging his preconceptions.

When he turned around, Calhoun was behind him. He felt somewhat as if he had been caught stealing jam. "Oh, hello, Doctor," he said quickly.

"How do you do, Major," Calhoun replied with deliberation. "May I inquire as to what is going on?"

"Certainly. I've sent Lieutenant Thomas out to reconnoiter."

"Lieutenant?"

26

"Brevet lieutenant. I was forced to use him for work far beyond his rank; I found it expedient to assign him the rank and pay of his new duties."

Calhoun pursued that point no further, but answered with another, in the same faintly critical tone of voice. "I suppose you realize that it jeopardizes all of us to send anyone outside? I am a little surprised that you should act in such a matter without consulting with others."

"I am sorry you feel that way about it, Colonel," Ardmore replied, in a conscious attempt to conciliate the older man, "but I am required to make the final decision in any case, and it is of prime importance to our task that nothing be permitted to distract your attention from your all-important job of research. Have you completed your experiment?" he went on quickly.

"Yes."

"Well?"

"The results were positive. The mice died."

"How about Wilkie?"

"Oh, Wilkie was unhurt, naturally. That is in accordance with my predictions."

Jefferson Thomas. Bachelor of Arts *magna cum laude*, University of California, Bachelor of Law, Harvard Law School, professional hobo, private and cook's helper, and now a brevet lieutenant, intelligence, United States army, spent his first night outside shivering on pine needles where dark had overtaken him. Early the next morning he located a ranchhouse.

They fed him, but they were anxious for him to move along. "You never can tell when one of those heathens is going to come snooping around," apologized his host, "and I can't afford to be arrested for harboring refugees. I got the wife and kids to think about." But he followed Thomas out to the road, still talking, his natural garrulity prevailing over his caution. He seemed to take a grim pleasure in bewailing the catastrophe.

"God knows what I'm raising those kids up to. Some nights it seems like the only reasonable thing to do is to put them all out of their sorrow. But Jessie—that's my wife—says it's a scandal and a sin to talk that way, that the Lord will take care of things all in His own good time. Maybe so—but I know it's no favor to a child to raise it up to be bossed around and lorded over by those monkeys." He spat. "It's not American."

"What's this about penalties for harboring refugees?"

The rancher stared at him. "Where've you been, friend?"

"Up in the hills. I haven't laid eyes on one of the so-and-so's yet."

"You will. But then you haven't got a number, have you? You'd better get one. No, that won't do you any good; you'd just land in a labor camp if you tried to get one."

"Number?"

"Registration number. Like this." He pulled a glassine-covered card out of his pocket and displayed it. It had affixed to it a poor but recognizable picture of the rancher, his fingerprints, and pertinent data as to his occupation, marital status, address, etcetera. There was a long, hyphenated number running across the top. The rancher indicated it with a work-stained finger. "That first part is my number. It means I have permission from the emperor to stay alive and enjoy the air and sunshine," he added bitterly. "The second part is my serial classification. It tells where I live and what I do. If I want to cross the county line, I have to have that changed. If I want to go to any other town than the one I'm assigned to do my marketing in, I've got to get a day's special permit. Now I ask you—is that any way for a man to live?"

"Not for me," agreed Thomas. "Well, I guess I had better be on my way before I get you in trouble. Thanks for the breakfast."

"Don't mention it. It's a pleasure to do a favor for a fellow American these days."

He started off down the road at once, not wishing the kindly rancher to see how thoroughly he had been moved by the picture of his degradation. The implications of that registration card had shaken his free soul in a fashion that the simple, intellectual knowledge of the defeat of the United States had been unable to do.

He moved slowly for the first two or three days, avoiding the towns until he had gathered sufficient knowledge of the enforced new customs to be able to conduct himself without arousing suspicion. It was urgently desirable that he be able to enter at least one big city in order to snoop around, read the bulletin boards, and find a chance to talk with persons whose occupations permitted them to travel. From a standpoint of personal safety he was quite willing to chance it without an indentification card but he remembered clearly a repeated injunction of

Ardmore's "Your paramount duty is to return! Don't go making a hero of yourself. Don't take any chance you can avoid and *come back!*"

Cities would have to wait.

Thomas skirted around towns at night, avoiding patrols as he used to avoid railroad cops. The second night out he found the first of his objectives, a hobos' jungle. It was just where he had expected to find it, from his recollection of previous trips through the territory. Nevertheless, he almost missed it, for the inevitable fire was concealed by a jury-rigged oil-can stove, and shielded from chance observation.

He slipped into the circle and sat down without comment, as custom required, and waited for them to look him over.

Presently a voice said plaintively: "It's Gentleman Jeff. Cripes, Jeff, you gave me a turn. I thought you was a flatface. Whatcha been doin' with yourself, Jeff?"

"Oh, one thing and another. On the dodge."

"Who isn't these days?" the voice returned. "Everywhere you try, those slant-eyes—" He broke into a string of attributions concerning the progenitors and personal habits of the PanAsians about which he could not possibly have had positive knowledge.

"Stow it, Moe," another voice commanded. "Tell us the news, Jeff."

"Sorry," Thomas refused affably, "but I've been up in the hills, kinda keeping out of the army and doing a little fishing."

"You should have stayed there. Things are bad everywhere. Nobody dares give an unregistered man a day's work and it takes everything you've got just to keep out of the labor camps. It makes the big Red hunt look like a picnic."

"Tell me about the labor camps," Thomas suggested. "I might get hungry enough to try one for a while."

"You don't know. Nobody *could* get that hungry." The voice paused, as if the owner were turning the unpleasant subject over in his mind. "Did you know the Seattle Kid?"

"Seem to recall. Little squint-eyed guy, handy with his hands?"

"That's him. Well, he was in one, maybe a week, and got out. Couldn't tell us how; his mind was gone. I saw him the night he died. His body was a mass of sores, blood poisoning, I guess." He paused. then added reflectively: "The smell was pretty bad."

Thomas wanted to drop the subject but he needed to know more. "Who gets sent to these camps?"

"Any man that isn't already working at an approved job. Boys from fourteen on up. All that was left alive of the army after we folded up. Anybody that's caught without a registration card."

"That ain't the half of it," added Moe. "You should see what they do with unassigned women. Why, a woman was telling me just the other day—a nice old gal; gimme a handout. She was telling me about her niece used to be a schoolteacher, and the flatfaces don't want any American schools or teachers. When they registered her they—"

"Shut up, Moe. You talk too much."

*　　*　　*

It was disconnected, fragmentary, the more so as he was rarely able to ask direct questions concerning the things he really wanted to know. Nevertheless he gradually built up a picture of a people being systematically and thoroughly enslaved, a picture of a nation as helpless as a man completely paralyzed, its defenses destroyed, its communications entirely in the hands of the invaders.

Everywhere he found boiling resentment, a fierce willingness to fight against the tyranny, but it was undirected, uncoordinated, and, in any modern sense, unarmed. Sporadic rebellion was as futile as the scurrying of ants whose hill has been violated. PanAsians could be killed, yes, and there were men willing to shoot on sight, even in the face of the certainty of their own deaths. But their hands were bound by the greater certainty of brutal multiple retaliation against their own kind. As with the Jews in Germany before the final blackout in Europe, bravery was not enough, for one act of violence against the tyrants would be paid for by other men, women, and children at unspeakable compound interest.

Even more distressing than the miseries he saw and heard about were the reports of the planned elimination of the American culture as such. The schools were closed. No word might be printed in English. There was a suggestion of a time, one generation away, when English would be an illiterate language, used orally alone by helpless peons who would never be able to revolt for sheer lack of a means of communication on any wide scale.

It was impossible to form any rational estimate of the numbers of Asiatics now in the United States.

Transports, it was rumored, arrived daily on the West coast, bringing thousands of administrative civil servants, most of whom were veterans of the amalgamation of India. Whether or not they could be considered as augmenting the armed forces who had conquered and now policed the country it was difficult to say, but it was evident that they would replace the white minor officials who now assisted in civil administration at pistol point. When those white officials were "eliminated" it would be still more difficult to organize resistance.

Thomas found the means to enter the cities in one of the hobo jungles.

Finny—surname unknown—was not, properly speaking, a knight of the road, but one who had sought shelter among them and who paid his way by practicing his talent. He was an old anarchist comrade who had served his concept of freedom by engraving really quite excellent Federal Reserve notes without complying with the formality of obtaining permission from the treasury department. Some said that his name had been Phineas; others connected his monicker with his preference for manufacturing five-dollar bills—"big enough to be useful; not big enough to arouse suspicion."

He made a registration card for Thomas at the request of one of the 'bos. He talked while Thomas watched him work. "It's only the registration number that we really have to worry about, son. Practically none of the Asiatics you will run into can read English, so it really doesn't matter a lot we say about you. 'Mary had a little lamb—' would probably do.

Same for the photograph. To them, all white men look alike." He picked up a handful of assorted photographs from his kit and peered at them nearsightedly through thick spectacles. "Here—pick out one of these that looks not unlike you and we will use it. Now for the number—"

The old man's hands were shaky, almost palsied, yet they steadied down to a deft sureness as he transferred India ink to cardboard in amazing simulation of machine printing. And this he did without proper equipment, without precision tools, under primitive conditions. Thomas understood why the old artist's masterpieces caused headaches for bank clerks. "There!" he announced. "I've given you a serial number which states that you were registered shortly after the change, and a classification number which permits you to travel. It also says that you are physically unfit for manual labor, and are permitted to peddle or beg. It's the same thing to their minds."

"Thanks, awfully," said Thomas. "Now . . . uh . . . what do I owe you for this?"

Finny's reaction made him feel as if he had uttered some indecency. "Don't mention payment, my son! Money is wrong—it's the means whereby man enslaves his brother."

"I beg your pardon, sir," Thomas apologized sincerely. "Nevertheless, I wish there were some way for me to do something for you."

"That is another matter. Help your brother when you can, and help will come to you when you need it."

Thomas found the old anarchist's philosophy confused, confusing, and impractical, but he spent considerable time drawing him out, as he seemed to know more about the PanAsians than anyone else he had met. Finny seemed unafraid of them and completely confident of his own ability to cope with them when necessary. Of all the persons Thomas had met since the change, Finny seemed the least disturbed by it—in fact, disturbed not at all, and completely lacking in any emotion of hate or bitterness. This was hard for him to understand at first in a person as obviously warm-hearted as Finny, but he came to realize that, since the anarchist believed that all government was wrong and that all men were to him in *fact* brothers, the difference to him was one of degree only. Looking at the PanAsians through Finny's eyes there was nothing to hate; they were simply more misguided souls whose excesses were deplorable.

Thomas did not see it from such Olympian detachment. The PanAsians were murdering and oppressing a once-free people. A good PanAsian was a dead PanAsian, he told himself, until the last one was driven back across the Pacific. If Asia was overpopulated, let them limit their birth rate.

Nevertheless, Finny's detachment and freedom from animus enabled Thomas more nearly to appreciate the nature of the problem. "Don't make the mistake of thinking of the PanAsians as *bad*—they're not—but they *are* different. Behind their arrogance is a racial inferiority complex, a mass paranoia, that makes it necessary for them to prove to themselves by proving to us that a yellow man is just as good as a white man, and a damned sight better. Remember that, son, they want the outward signs of respect more than they want anything else in the world."

"But why should they have an inferiority complex about us? We've been completely out of touch with them for more than two generations—ever since the Nonintercourse Act."

"Do you think racial memory is that short-lived? The seeds of this are way back in the nineteenth century. Do you recall that two high Japanese officials had to commit honorable suicide to wipe out a slight that was done Commodore Perry when he opened up Japan? Now those two deaths are being paid for by the deaths of thousands of American officials."

"But the PanAsians aren't Japanese."

"No, and they are not Chinese. They are a mixed race, strong, proud, and prolific. From the American standpoint they have the vices of both and the virtues of neither. But from my standpoint they are simply human beings, who have been duped into the old fallacy of the State as a super-entity. *'Ich habe einen Kameraden.'* Once you understand the nature of—" He went off into a long dissertation, a mixture of Rousseau, Rocker, Thoreau, and others. Thomas found it inspirational, but unconvincing.

But the discussion with Finny was of real use to Thomas in comprehending what they were up against. The Nonintercourse Act had kept the American people from knowing anything important about their enemy. Thomas wrinkled his brow, trying to recall what he knew about the history of it.

At the time it had been passed, the Act had been no more than a *de jure* recognition of a *de facto* condition. The sovietizing of Asia had excluded westerners, particularly Americans, from Asia more effectively than could any Act of Congress. The obscure reasons that had led the Congress of that period to think that the United States gained in dignity by passing a law confirming what the commissars had already done to us baffled Thomas; it smacked of Sergeant Dogberry's policy toward thieves. He supposed that it had simply seemed cheaper to wish Red Asia out of existence than to fight a war.

The policy behind the Act had certainly seemed to justify itself for better than half a century; there had been no war. The proponents of the measure had maintained that China was a big bite even for Soviet Russia to digest and that the United States need fear no war while the digesting was taking place. They had been correct as far as they went—but as a result of the Nonintercourse Act we had our backs turned when *China* digested Russia . . . leaving America to face a system even stranger to western ways of thinking than had been the Soviet system it displaced.

On the strength of the forged registration card and Finny's coaching as to the etiquette of being a serf, Thomas ventured into a medium-sized city. The cleverness of Finny's work was put to test almost immediately.

He had stopped at a street corner to read a posted notice. It was a general order to all Americans to be present at a television receiver at eight each evening in order to note any instructions that their rulers might have for them. It was not news; the order had been in effect for some days and he had heard of it. He was about to turn away when he felt a sharp, stinging blow across his shoulder blades. He whirled around and found himself facing a PanAsian wearing the green uniform of a civil administrator and carrying a swagger cane.

"Keep out of the way, boy!" He spoke in English, but in a light, singing tone which lacked the customary American accentuation.

Thomas jumped into the gutter—"They like to look down, not up"—and clasped his hands together in the form required. He ducked his head and replied, "The master speaks; the servant obeys."

"That's better," acknowledged the Asiatic, apparently somewhat mollified. "Your ticket."

The man's accent was not bad, but Thomas did not comprehend immediately, possibly because the emotional impact of his experience in the role of slave was all out of proportion to what he had expected. To say that he raged inwardly is meaninglessly inadequate.

The swagger cane cut across his face. "Your ticket!"

Thomas produced his registration card. The time the Oriental spent in examining it gave Thomas an opportunity to pull himself together to some extent. At the moment he did not care greatly whether the card passed muster or not; if it came to trouble, he would take this one apart with his bare hands.

But it passed. The Asiatic grudgingly handed it back and strutted away, unaware that death had brushed his elbow.

It turned out that there was little to be picked up in town that he had not already acquired second-hand in the hobo jungles. He had a chance to estimate for himself the proportion of rulers to ruled, and saw for himself that the schools were closed and the newspapers had vanished. He noted with interest that church services were still held, although any other gathering together of white men in assembly was strictly forbidden.

But it was the dead, wooden faces of the people, the quiet children, that got under his skin and made him decide to sleep in the jungles rather than in town.

Thomas ran across an old friend at one of the hobo hideouts. Frank Roosevelt Mitsui was as American as Will Rogers, and much more American than that English aristocrat, George Washington. His grandfather had brought his grandmother, half Chinese and half wahini, from Honolulu to Los Angeles, where he opened a nursery and raised flowers, plants, and little yellow children, children that knew neither Chinese nor Japanese, nor cared.

Frank's father met his mother, Thelma Wang, part Chinese but mostly Caucasian, at the International Club at the University of Southern California. He took her to the Imperial Valley and installed her on a nice ranch with a nice mortgage. By the time Frank was raised, so was the mortgage.

Jeff Thomas had cropped lettuce and honeydew melon for Frank Mitsui three seasons and knew him as a good boss. He had become almost intimate with his employer because of his liking for the swarm of brown kids that were Frank's most important crop. But the sight of a flat, yellow face in a hobo jungle made Thomas' hackles rise and almost interfered with his recognizing his old acquaintance.

It was an awkward meeting. Well as he knew Frank, Thomas was in no mood to trust an Oriental. It was Frank's eyes that convinced him; they held a tortured look that was even more intense than that found in the eyes of white men, a look that did not lessen even while he smiled and shook hands.

"Well, Frank," Jeff improvised inanely, "who'd expect to find you here? I should think you'd find it easy to get along with the new regime."

Frank Mitsui looked still more unhappy and seemed to be fumbling for words. One of the other hobos cut in. "Don't be a fool, Jeff. Don't you *know* what they've done to people like Frank?"

"No, I don't."

"Well, you're on the dodge. If they catch you, it's the labor camp. So is Frank. But if they catch *him*, it's curtains—right now. They'll shoot him on sight."

"So? What did you do, Frank?"

Mitsui shook his head miserably.

"He didn't do anything," the other continued. "The empire has no use for American Asiatics. They're liquidating them."

It was quite simple. The Pacific coast Japanese, Chinese, and the like did not fit into the pattern of serfs and overlords—particularly the half-breeds. They were a danger to the stability of the pattern. With cold logic they were being hunted down and killed.

Thomas listened to Frank's story. "When I got home they were dead—all of them. My little Shirley, Junior, Jimmy, the baby—and Alice." He put his face in his hands and wept. Alice was his wife. Thomas remembered her as a brown, stocky woman in overalls and straw hat, who talked very little but smiled a lot.

"At first I thought I would kill myself," Mitsui went on when he had sufficient control of himself, "then I knew better. I hid in an irrigation ditch for two days, and then I got away over the mountains. Then some whites almost killed me before I could convince them I was on their side."

Thomas could understand how that would happen, and could think of nothing to say. Frank was damned two ways; there was no hope for him. "What do you intend to do now, Frank?"

He saw a sudden return of the will to live in the man's face. "That is why I will not let myself die! Ten for each one"—he counted them off on his brown fingers—"ten of those devils for each one of my babies—and twenty for Alice. Then maybe ten more for myself, and I can die."

"Hm-m-m. Any luck?"

"Thirteen, so far. It is slow, for I have to be very sure, so that they won't kill me before I finish."

Thomas pondered it in his mind, trying to fit this new knowledge into his own purpose. Such fixed determination should be useful, if directed. But it was some hours later before he approached Mitsui again.

"How would you," he asked gently, "like to raise your quota from ten to a thousand each—two thousand for Alice?"

41

CHAPTER THREE

THE EXTERIOR ALARMS BROUGHT ARDMORE TO THE
portal long before Thomas whistled the tune that
activated the door. Ardmore watched the door by
televisor from the guard room, his thumb resting on
a control, ready to burn out of existence any unexpected visitor. When he saw Thomas enter his thumb
relaxed, but at the sight of his companion it tight-
ened again. A PanAsian! He almost blasted them in
sheer reflex before he checked himself. It was possible, barely possible, that Thomas had brought a prisoner to question.

"Major! Major Ardmore! It's Thomas."

"Stand where you are. Both of you."

"It's all right, Major. He's an American. I vouch
for him."

"Maybe." The voice that reached Thomas over the
announcing phone was still grimly suspicious. "Just

the same—peel off all of your clothes, both of you."
They did so, Thomas biting his lip in humiliation,
Mitsui trembling in agitation. He did not understand
it and he felt trapped. "Now turn around slowly and
let me look you over," the voice commanded.

Having satisfied himself that they were unarmed,
Ardmore told them to stand still and wait, then
called Graham on the intercommunication circuit.
"Graham!"

"Yes, sir."

"Report to me at once in the guard room."

"But, Major, I can't. Dinner will be—"

"Never mind dinner! Move!"

"Yes, sir!"

Ardmore pointed out the situation to him in the
screen. "You go down there and handcuff both of
them from behind. Secure the Asiatic first. Make
him back up to you, and watch yourself. If he tries to
jump you, I may have to wing you, too."

"I don't like this, Major," Graham protested.
"Thomas is all right. He wouldn't be up to any
hanky-panky."

"Sure, man, I know he's all right, too. But he may
be drugged and under control. This set-up could be
a Trojan Horse gag. Now get down and do as you are
told."

While Graham was gingerly carrying out his un-
welcome assignment—and making himself, in fact,
eligible for a Congressional Medal which he would
never receive, for his artist's imagination perceived
too clearly the potential danger and forced him to
call up courage for the task—Ardmore phoned Brooks.

"Doctor, can you drop what you are doing?"

"Why, perhaps I can. Yes, I may say so. What is it you wish?"

"Then come to my office. Thomas is back. I want to know whether or not he is under the influence of drugs."

"But I am not a medical man—"

"I know that, but you are the nearest thing we've got to one."

"Very well, sir."

Dr. Brooks examined Thomas' pupils, tried his knee jerks, and checked his pulse and respiration. "I should say that he was perfectly normal, though exhausted and laboring under excitement. Naturally, this is not a positive diagnosis. If I had more time—"

"It will do for now. Thomas, I trust you won't hold it against me if we leave you locked up until we have examined your Asiatic pal."

"Certainly not, Major," Thomas told him with a wry grin, "since you're going to, anyhow."

Frank Mitsui's flesh quivered and sweat dripped from his face when Brooks stuck the hypodermic into him, but he did not draw away. Presently he relaxed under the influence of the drug that releases inhibitions, and strips from the speech centers the protection of cortical censorship. His face became peaceful.

But it was not peaceful a few minutes later when they began to question him, nor was there peace in any of their faces. This was truth, too raw and too brutal for any man to stand. Deep lines carved themselves from nose to jaw in Ardmore's face as he listened to the little man's pitiful story. No matter what line they started him on, he always came back to the scene of his dead children, his broken household. Finally Ardmore put a stop to it.

"Give him the antidote, doc. I can't stand any more of this. I've found out all I need to know."

Ardmore shook hands with him solemnly after he had returned to full awareness. "We are glad to have you with us, Mr. Mitsui. And we'll put you to some work that will give you a chance to get some of your own back. Right now I want Dr. Brooks to give you a soporific that will let you get about sixteen hours' sleep; then we can think about swearing you in and what kind of work you can be most useful doing."

"I don't need any sleep, Mister . . . Major."

"Just the same, you are going to get some. And so is Thomas, as soon as he has reported. In fact—" He broke off and studied the apparently impassive face. "In fact, I want you to take a sleeping pill every night. Those are orders. You'll draw them from me and take them in my presence every night before you go to bed." There are certain bonus advantages to military absolutism. Ardmore could not tolerate the idea of the little yellow man lying awake and staring at the ceiling.

Brooks and Graham would quite plainly have liked to stay and hear Thomas' report, but Ardmore refused to notice the evident fact and dismissed them. He wished first to evaluate the data himself.

"Well, Lieutenant, I'm damn glad you're back."

"I'm glad to be back. Did you say 'lieutenant'? I assume that my rank reverts."

"Why should it? As a matter of fact, I am trying to figure out a plausible reason for commissioning Graham and Scheer. It would simplify things around here to eliminate social differences. But that is a side issue. Let's hear what you've done. I suppose you've come back with all our problems solved and tied up with string?"

"Not likely." Thomas grinned and relaxed.

"I didn't expect it. But seriously, between ourselves, I've got to pull something out of the hat, and it's got to be good. The scientific staff is beginning to crowd me, particularly Colonel Calhoun. There's no damn sense in their making miracles in the laboratory unless I can dope out some way to apply those miracles in strategy and tactics."

"Have they really gone so far?"

"You'd be surprised. They've taken that so-called 'Ledbetter effect' and shaken it the way a terrier shakes a rat. They can do anything with it but peel the potatoes and put out the cat."

"Really?"

"Really."

"What sort of things can they do?"

"Well—" Ardmore took a deep breath. "Honestly, I don't know where to begin. Wilkie has tried to keep me posted with simplified explanations, but, between ourselves, I didn't understand more than every other word. One way of putting it is to say that they've discovered atomic control—oh, I don't mean atom-splitting, or artificial radioactivity. Look—we speak of space, and time, and matter, don't we?"

"Yes. There's Einstein's space-time concept, of course."

"Of course. Space-time is standard stuff in high school these days. But these men really *mean* it. They really mean that space and time and mass and

47

energy and radiation and gravity are all simply different ways of thinking about the *same thing*. And if you once catch on to how just one of them works, you have the key to all of them. According to Wilkie, physicists up to now, even after the A-bomb was developed, were just fooling around the edges of the subject; they had the beginnings of a unified field theory, but they didn't really believe it themselves; they usually acted as if these were all as different as the names for them.

"Apparently Ledbetter hit on the real meaning of radiation, and that has given Calhoun and Wilkie the key to everything else in physics. Is that clear?" he added with a grin.

"Not very," Thomas admitted. "Can you give me some idea of what they can *do* with it?"

"Well, to begin with, the original Ledbetter effect—the thing that killed most of the personnel here—Wilkie calls an accidental side issue. Brooks says that the basic radiation affected the colloidal dispersal of living tissue; those that were killed were coagulated by it. It might just as well have been set to release surface tension—in fact, they did that the other day, exploded a half of beefsteak like so much dynamite."

"Huh?"

"Don't ask me how; I'm just repeating the explanation given me. But the point is, they seem to have found out what makes matter tick. They can explode it—sometimes—and use it for a source of power. They can transmute it into any element they want. They seem to be confident that they know what to do to find out how gravity works, so that they will be able to handle gravity the way we now handle electricity."

"I thought gravity was not considered a force in the modern concepts."

"So it isn't—but, then, 'force' isn't force, either, in unified field theory. Hell's bells, you've got me bogged down in language difficulties. Wilkie says that mathematics is the only available language for these ideas."

"Well, I guess I'll just have to get along without understanding it. But, frankly, I don't see how they managed to come so far so fast. That changes just about everything we thought we knew. Honestly, how is it that it took a hundred fifty years to go from Newton to Edison, yet these boys can knock out results like that in a few weeks?"

"I don't know myself. The same point occurred to me, and I asked Calhoun about it. He informed me in that schoolmaster way of his that it was because those pioneers did not have the tensor calculus, vector analysis, and matrix algebra."

"Well, I wouldn't know," observed Thomas. "They don't teach that stuff in law school."

"Nor me," admitted Ardmore. "I tried looking over some of their work sheets. I can do simple algebra, and I've had some calculus, though I haven't used it for years, but I couldn't make sense out of this stuff. It looked like Sanskrit; most of the signs were different, and even the old ones didn't seem to mean the same things. Look—I thought that a times b always equaled b times a."

"Doesn't it?"

"Not when these boys get through kicking it around.

But we are getting way off the subject. Bring me up to date."

"Yes, sir." Jeff Thomas talked steadily for a long time, trying very hard to paint a detailed picture of everything he had seen and heard and felt. Ardmore did not interrupt him except with questions intended to clarify points. There was a short silence when he had concluded. Finally Ardmore said:

"I think I must have had a subconscious belief that you would come back with some piece of information that would fall right into place and tell me what to do. But I don't see much hope in what you have told me. How to win back a country that is as completely paralyzed and as carefully guarded as you describe the United States to be is beyond me."

"Of course, I didn't see the whole country. About two hundred miles from here is as far as I got."

"Yes, but you got reports from the other hobos that covered the whole country, didn't you?"

"Yes."

"And it was all about the same. I think we can safely assume that what you heard, confirmed by what you saw, gives a fairly true picture. How recent do you suppose was the dope you got by the grapevine telegraph?"

"Well—maybe three or four days old news from the East coast—no more than that."

"That seems reasonable. News always travels by the fastest available route. It's certainly not very encouraging. And yet—" He paused and scowled in evident puzzlement. "And yet I have a feeling that you said something that was the key to the whole matter. I can't put my finger on it. I began to get an

50

idea while you were talking, then some other point came up and diverted my mind, and I lost it."

"Maybe it would help if I started in again at the beginning," suggested Thomas.

"No need to. I'll play the recording back piece by piece sometime tomorrow, if I don't think of it in the meantime."

They were interrupted by peremptory knocking at the door. Ardmore called out, "Come in!" Colonel Calhoun entered.

"Major Ardmore, what's this about a PanAsiatic prisoner?"

"Not quite that, Colonel, but we do have an Asiatic here now. He's American-born."

Calhoun brushed aside the distinction. "Why wasn't I informed? I have notified you that I urgently require a man of Mongolian blood for test experimentation."

"Doctor, with the skeleton staff we have, it is difficult to comply with all the formalities of military etiquette. You were bound to learn of it in the ordinary course of events—in fact, it seems that you *were* informed in some fashion."

Calhoun snorted. "Through the casual gossip of subordinates!"

"I'm sorry, Colonel, but it couldn't be helped. Just at the moment I am trying to receive Thomas' reconnaisance report."

"Very well, sir." Calhoun was icily formal. "Will you be good enough to have the Asiatic report to me at once?"

"I can't do that. He is asleep, drugged, and there

is no way to produce him for you before tomorrow. Besides, while I am quite sure that he will be entirely cooperative in any useful experimentation, he is an American citizen and a civilian under our protection—not a prisoner. We'll have to take it up with him."

Calhoun left as abruptly as he had come. "Jeff," mused Ardmore, glancing after him, "speaking strictly off the record—oh, strictly!—if there ever comes a time when we are no longer bound down by military necessity, I'm going to paste that old beezer right in the puss!"

"Why don't you clamp down on him?"

"I can't, and he knows it. He's invaluable, indispensable. We've absolutely got to have his brains for research, and you can't conscript brains just by handing out orders. Y'know, though, in spite of his brilliance, I sometimes think he's just a little bit cracked."

"Shouldn't be surprised. What does he want Frank Mitsui so bad for?"

"Well, that's somewhat involved. They've proved that the original Ledbetter effect depends on a characteristic of the life form involved—you might call it a natural frequency. It seems that everybody has his own wavelength, or wavelengths. The notion seemed like so much astrology to me, but Dr. Brooks says that it is not only the straight dope; it isn't even new. He showed me a paper by a chap named Fox, at the University of London, 'way back in 1945—Fox showed that each individual rabbit had hemoglobin with its own individual wavelength; it absorbed that wavelength in spectroscopic analysis, that one wavelength and no other. You could tell two rabbits apart with it, or you could tell a rabbit from a dog, simply by the spectra of their hemoglobins.

"This Dr. Fox tried to do the same thing with humans, but it didn't work—no distinguishable difference in wavelengths. But Calhoun and Wilkie have rigged a spectroscope for the spectrum Ledbetter was playing with, and *it* shows clearly separate wavelengths for each sample of human blood. Conversely, if they set up a tuned Ledbetter projector and start running down or up the scale, when they come to your individual, unique frequency, your red blood cells start absorbing energy, the hemoglobins protein breaks down and—*Spung!*—you're dead. I'm standing right beside you and I'm not even hurt; they haven't come to my frequency. Now Brooks has an idea that these frequencies come by groups according to races. He thinks they can tune it to discriminate by races, to knock over all the Asiatics in a group and not touch the white men, and vice versa."

Thomas shivered. "Whew! That *would* be a weapon."

"Yes, it would. It's just on paper so far, but they want to test it on Mitsui. As I gather what they intended to do, they don't intend to kill him, but it's bound to be dangerous as all hell to Mitsui."

"Frank won't mind chancing it," Thomas commented.

"No, I don't suppose he would." It seemed to Ardmore that it would probably be a favor to Mitsui to give him a clean, painless death in the laboratory. "Now about another matter. It seems to me we ought to be able to work up a sort of permanent secret service, using your hobo pals and their sources of information. Let's talk about it."

Ardmore gained a few days' respite in which to consider further the problem of military use of the weapons at his disposal while the research staff tested their theories concerning the interrelation between racial types and the improved Ledbetter effect. The respite did him no good. He had a powerful weapon, yes; in fact, many powerful weapons, for it seemed that the new principles they had tapped had fully as protean possibilities as electricity. It seemed extremely likely that if the United States defense forces had had, one year earlier, the tools now available in the Citadel, the United States would never have fallen.

But six men cannot whip an empire—not by brute force. The emperor could, if necessary, expend six million men to defeat six. The hordes of the empire could come at them barehanded and win, move over them as an avalanche moves, until they were buried under a mountain of dead flesh. Ardmore had to have an army to fight with his wonderful new weapons.

The question was: how to recruit and train such an army?

Certain it was that the PanAsians would not hold still while he went into the highways and byways and got his forces together. The thoroughness with which they had organized police surveillance of the entire population made it evident that they were acutely aware of the danger of revolution and would stamp out any such activity before it could possibly reach proportions dangerous to them.

There remained one clandestine group, the hobos.

He consulted with Thomas as to the possibility of organizing them for military purposes. Thomas shook his head at the idea.

"You can't understand the hobo temperament, Chief. There is not one in a hundred who could be depended on to observe the strict self-discipline necessary for such an enterprise. Suppose you were able to arm all of them with projectors—I don't say that is possible, but suppose you could—you still would not have an army; you would simply have an undisciplined rabble."

"Wouldn't they fight?"

"Oh, sure, they'd fight. They'd fight as individuals, and they would do quite a bit of slaughter until some flatface caught them off guard and winged them."

"I wonder if we can depend on them as sources of information."

"That's another matter. Most of the road kids won't have any idea that they are being used to obtain military information. I'll handpick not over a dozen to act as reporters to me, and I won't tell them anything they don't have to know."

Any way he looked at it, simple, straightforward military use of the new weapons was not expedient. Brutal frontal attack was for the commander who had men to expend. General U. S. Grant could afford to say, "I will fight it out on this line if it takes all summer," because he could lose three men to the enemy's one and still win. Those tactics were not for the commander who could not afford to lose *any* men. For him it must be deception, misdirection—feint and slash and run away—"and live to fight another day." The nursery rhyme finished itself in his mind. That was it. It had to be something totally unexpected, something that the PanAsians would not realize was warfare until they were overwhelmed by it.

It would have to be something like the "fifth columns" that destroyed the European democracies from within in the tragic days that led up to the final blackout of European civilization. But this would not be a fifth column of traitors, bent on paralyzing a free country, but the antithesis of that, a sixth column of patriots whose privilege it would be to destroy the morale of invaders, make them afraid, unsure of themselves.

And misdirection was the key to it, and art of fooling!

Ardmore felt a little better when he had reached that conclusion. It was something he could understand, a job suited to an advertising man. He had been trying to crack it as a military problem, but he was not a field marshal and it had been silly of him to try to make a noise like one. His mind did not work that way. This was primarily a job in publicity, a matter of mob psychology. A former boss of his, under whom he had learned the racket, used to tell him, "I can sell dead cats to the board of health with a proper budget and a free hand."

Well, he had a free hand, all right, and the budget was no problem. Of course, he could not use the newspapers and the old channels of advertising, but there would be a way. The problem now was to figure out the weak points of the PanAsians and decide how Calhoun's little gadgets could be used to play on those weak points until the PanAsians were sick of the whole deal and anxious to go home.

He did not have a plan as yet. When a man is at a loss for a course of action, he usually calls for a conference. Ardmore did.

He sketched out to them the situation up to date, including all that Thomas had learned and all that had come in by television through the conquerors' "educational" broadcasts. Then he discussed the powers that were made available to them by the research staff, and the various obvious ways in which they could be applied as military weapons, emphasizing the personnel necessary to use each type of weapon effectively. Having done so, he asked for suggestions.

"Do I understand, Major," Calhoun began, "that after rather pointedly telling us that you would make all military decisions you are now asking us to make up your mind for you?"

"Not at all, Colonel. I have still the responsibility for any decision, but this is a new sort of military situation. A suggestion from any source may prove valuable. I don't flatter myself that I have a monopoly on common sense, nor on originality. I would like for every one of us to tackle this problem and let the others criticize it."

"Do you yourself have any plan to offer us?"

"I am reserving my opinions until the rest of you have spoken."

"Very well, sir"—Dr. Calhoun straightened himself up—"since you have asked for it, I will tell you what I think should be done in this situation—what, in fact, is the only thing that can be done.

"You are aware of the tremendous power of the

forces I have made available." Ardmore noticed Wilkie's mouth tighten at this allocation of credit, but neither of them interrupted. "In your résumé, you underestimated them, if anything. We have a dozen fast scout cars housed here in the Citadel. By refitting them with power units of the Calhoun type they can be made faster than anything the enemy can put into the air. We will mount on them the heaviest projectors and attack. With overwhelmingly superior weapons it is only a matter of time until we will have the PanAsiatic empire beaten to its knees!"

Ardmore wondered how any man could be so blind. He did not himself wish to argue against Calhoun; he said, "Thank you, Colonel. I'll ask you to submit that plan written up in more detail. In the meantime does anyone wish to amplify or criticize the colonel's suggestion?" He waited hopefully, then added, "Come now, no plan is perfect. You must have some details to add, at least."

Graham took the plunge. "How often do you expect to come down to eat?"

Calhoun cut in before Ardmore could call on him. "Well, I'm damned! I must say that I consider this no time for facetiousness."

"Wait a minute," protested Graham, "I didn't mean to be funny. I'm quite serious. That's my department. Those scout cars are not equipped to keep the air very long, and it seems to me that it will take quite a long time to reconquer the United States with a dozen scout cars, even if we located enough men to keep them in the air all the time. That means you have to come back to base to eat."

"Yes, and that means the base will have to be held against attack," Scheer put in suddenly.

"The base can be defended with other projectors." Calhoun's tone was scornful. "Major, I really must ask that the discussion be confined to sensible issues."

Ardmore rubbed his chin and said nothing.

Randall Brooks, who had been listening thoughtfully, pulled a piece of paper out of his pocket and began to sketch. "I think Scheer has something, Dr. Calhoun. If you will look here for a moment—here, at this point, is your base. The PanAsians can encircle the base with ships at a distance greater than the range of the base projectors. The greater speed of your scout cars will be unimportant, for the enemy can well afford to use as many ships as necessary to insure our craft not getting past the blockade. It's sure that the scout cars will have the projectors with which to fight, but they can't fight a hundred ships at once, and the enemies' weapons are powerful, too—we mustn't forget that."

"You're right they're powerful!" added Wilkie. "We can't afford to have a known base. With their bombardment rockets they could stand back a thousand miles and blow this whole mountain out of the ground, *if* they knew we were under it."

Calhoun stood up. "I'm not going to remain here and listen to misgivings of pusillanimous fools. My plan assumed that *men* would execute it." He walked stiffly out of the room.

Ardmore ignored his departure and went hurriedly on, "The objections made to Colonel Calhoun's scheme seem to me to apply to every plan for open, direct combat at this time. I have considered several and rejected them for approximately those reasons, at least for reasons of logistics—that is to say, the problem of military supply. However, I may not have thought of some perfectly feasible solution. Does anyone have a direct warfare method to suggest, a method which will not risk personnel?"

No one answered. "Very well, bring it up later if you think of one. It seems to me that we must necessarily work by misdirection. If we can't fight the enemy directly at *this time,* we must fool 'em until we can."

"I see," agreed Dr. Brooks, "the bull wears himself out on the cape and never sees the sword."

"Exactly. Exactly. I only wish it were as easy as that. Now do any of you have any ideas as to how we can use what we've got without letting them know who we are, where we are, or how many we are? And now I'm going to take time out for a cigarette while you think about it."

Presently, he added, "You might bear in mind that we have two real advantages: the enemy apparently has not the slightest idea that we even exist, and our weapons are strange to them, even mysterious. Wilkie, didn't you compare the Ledbetter effect to magic?"

"I should hope to shout, Chief! It's safe to say that, aside from the instruments in our laboratories, there just isn't any way in existence to detect the forces we are working with now. You don't even know they're *there*. It's like trying to hear radio with your bare ears."

"That's what I mean. Mysterious. Like the Indians when they first met up with the white man's firearms, they died and they didn't know why. Think about it. I'll shut up and let you."

Graham produced the first suggestion. "Major?"

"Yes?"

"Why couldn't we kidnap 'em?"

"How do you mean?"

"Well, your idea is to throw a scare into 'em, isn't it? How about a surprise raiding party, using the Ledbetter effect. We could go in one of the scout cars at night and pick out some really big shot, maybe the prince royal himself. We knock out everybody we come in contact with with the projectors, and we walk right in and snatch him."

"Any opinions about that, gentlemen?" Ardmore said, reserving his own.

"It seems to have something to it," commented Brooks. "I would suggest that the projectors be set to render unconscious for a number of hours rather than to kill. It seems to me that the psychological effect would be heightened if they simply awoke and found their big man gone. One has no recollection of what has happened under such circumstances, as Wilkie and Mitsui can testify."

"Why stop at the prince royal?" Wilkie wanted to know. "We could set up four raiding parties, two to a car, and make maybe twelve raids in a single night. That way we could knock over enough of their number-one men to really cause some disorganization."

"That seems like a good idea," Ardmore agreed. "We may not be able to pull off these raids more than once. If we could do enough damage right at the top in one blow, we might both demoralize them and set off a general uprising. What's the matter, Mitsui?"

He had noticed the Oriental looking unhappy as the plan was developed. Mitsui spoke reluctantly, "It will not work, I am afraid."

"You mean we can't kidnap them that way? Do you know something we don't about their guard methods?"

"No, no. With a force that reaches through walls and knocks a man down before he knows you are there I believe you can capture them, all right. But the results will not be as you foresee them."

"Why not?"

"Because you will gain no advantage. They will not assume that you are holding their chief men as prisoners; they will assume that each one has committed suicide. The results will be horrible."

It was purely a psychological point, with room for difference of opinion. But the white men could not believe that the PanAsians would dare to retaliate if it were made unmistakably plain to them that their sacred leaders were not dead, but at the mercy of captors. Besides, it was a plan that offered immediate action, which they were spoiling for. Ardmore finally agreed to its adoption for want of something better, although he had a feeling of misgiving which he suppressed.

For the next few days all effort was bent toward preparing the scout cars for the projected task. Scheer performed Herculean mechanical jobs, working eighteen and twenty hours a day, with the others working joyfully under his supervision. Calhoun even came off his high horse and agreed to take part in the raid, although he did not help with the "menial" work. Thomas went out on a quick scouting trip and made certain of the location of twelve well-scattered PanAsian seats of government.

In the buoyancy of spirit which resulted from a plan of campaign, *any* plan of campaign, Ardmore failed to remember his own decision that what was required was a sixth column, an underground, or at least, unsuspected organization which would demoralize the enemy from within. This present plan was not such a one, but an essentially military plan. He began to think of himself as, if not Napoleon, at least as a modern Swamp Rat, or Sandino, striking through the night at the professional soldiers and fading away.

But Mitsui was right.

The television receiver was used regularly, with full recording, to pick up anything that the overlords had to broadcast to their slaves. It had become something of a custom to meet in the common room at eight in the evening to listen to the regular broadcast in which new orders were announced to the population. Ardmore encouraged it; the "hate session" it inspired was, he believed, good for morale.

Two nights before the projected raid they were gathered as usual. The ugly, broad face of the usual propaganda artist was quickly replaced by another and older PanAsian whom he introduced as the "heavenly custodian of peace and order." The older man came quickly to the point. The American servants of a provincial government had committed the hideous sin of rebelling against their wise rulers and had captured the sacred person of the governor and held him prisoner in his own palace. The soldiers of the heavenly emperor had brushed aside the insane profaners in the course of which the governor had most regrettably gone to his ancestors.

A period of mourning was announced, commencing at once, which would be inaugurated by permitting the people of the province to expiate the sins of their cousins. The television scene cut from the room from which he spoke.

It came to rest on great masses of humanity, men, women, children, huddled, jammed, behind barbed wire. The pick-up came down close enough to permit the personnel of the Citadel to see the blind misery on the faces of the crowd, the wept-out children, the mothers carrying babies, the helpless fathers.

They did not have to watch those faces long. The pick-up panned over the packed mob, acre on acre of helpless human animals, then returned to a steady close-up of one section.

They used the epileptigenic ray on them. Now they no longer resembled anything human. It was, instead, as if tens of thousands of monstrous chickens had had their necks wrung all at once and had been thrown into the same pen to jerk out their death spasms. Bodies bounded into the air in bone-breaking, spine-smashing fits. Mothers threw their infants from them, or crushed them in uncontrollable, viselike squeeze.

The scene cut back to the placid face of the Asiatic dignitary. He announced with what seemed to be regret in his voice that penance for sins was not sufficient, it was necessary also to be educational, in this case to the extent of one in every thousand.

Ardmore did a quick calculation in his head. A hundred fifty thousand people! It was unbelievable.

But it was soon believed. The pick-up cut again, this time to a residential street in an American city. It followed a squad of PanAsian soldiers into the living room of a family. They were gathered about a television receiver, plainly stunned by what they had just seen. The mother was huddling a young girl child to her shoulder, trying to quiet her hysteria. They seemed stupefied, rather than frightened, when the soldiers burst into their home. The father produced his card without argument; the squad leader compared it with a list, and the soldiers attended to him.

They had evidently been instructed to use a method of killing that was not pretty.

Ardmore shut off the receiver. "The raid is off," he announced. "Go to bed, all of you. And each of you take a sleeping pill tonight. That's an order!"

They left at once. No one said anything. After they were gone, Ardmore turned the receiver back on and watched it through to the end. Then he sat alone for a long time, trying to get his thoughts back into coherence. Those who order sleeping drafts won't take them.

CHAPTER FOUR

ARDMORE KEPT VERY MUCH TO HIMSELF FOR THE NEXT two days, taking his meals in his quarters, and refusing anything but the briefest interviews, He saw his error plainly enough now; it was small solace to him that it had been another's mistake which had resulted in the massacre—he felt symbolically guilty.

But the problem remained with him. He knew now that he had been right when he had decided on a sixth column. A sixth column! Something which would conform in every superficial way to the pattern set up by the rulers, yet which would have in it the means of their eventual downfall. It might take years, but there must be no repetition of the ghastly mistake of direct action.

He knew intuitively that somewhere in Thomas' report was the idea he needed. He played it back again and again, but still he couldn't get it, even though he now knew it by heart. "They are systematically stamping out everything that is typically American in culture. The schools are gone, so are the newspapers. It is a capital offense to print anything in English. They have announced the early establishment of a system of translators for all business correspondence into their language; in the meantime all mail must be approved as necessary. All meetings are forbidden except religious meetings."

"I suppose that is a result of their experience in India. Keeps the slaves quiet." That was his own voice, sounding strange in reproduction.

"I suppose so, sir. Isn't it an historical fact that all successful empires have tolerated the local religions, no matter what else they suppressed?"

"I suppose so. Go ahead."

"The real strength of their system, I believe, is in their method of registration. They apparently were all set to put it into force, and pressed forward on that to the exclusion of other matters. It's turned the United States into one big prison camp in which it is almost impossible to move or communicate without permission from the jailers."

Words, words, and more words! He had played them over so many times that the significance was almost lost. Perhaps there was nothing in the report, after all—nothing but his imagination.

He responded to a knock at the door. It was Thomas. "They asked me to speak to you, sir," he said diffidently.

"What about?"

"Well—they are all gathered in the common room. They'd like to talk with you."

Another conference—and not of his choosing, this time. Well, he would have to go. "Tell them I will be in shortly."

"Yes, sir."

After Thomas had gone, he sat for a moment, then went to a drawer and took out his service side arm. He could smell mutiny in the very fact that someone had dared to call a general meeting without his permission. He buckled it on, then tried the slide and the change, and stood looking at it. Presently he unbuckled it and put it back into the drawer. It wouldn't help him in this mess.

He entered, sat down in his chair at the head of the table, and waited.

"Well?"

Brooks glanced around to see if anyone else wished to answer, cleared his throat, and said, "Uh—we wanted to ask you if you had any plan for us to follow."

"I do not have—as yet."

"Then we do have!" It was Calhoun.

"Yes, Colonel?"

"There is no sense in hanging around here with our hands tied. We have the strongest weapons the world has ever seen, but they need men to operate them."

"Well?"

"We are going to evacuate and go to South America! There we can find a government which will be interested in superior weapons."

"What good will that do the United States?"

"It's obvious. The empire undoubtedly intends to

extend its sway over this entire hemisphere. We can interest them in a preventive war. Or perhaps we can raise up an army of refugees."

"No!"

"I am afraid you can't help yourself, Major." The tone held malicious satisfaction.

He turned to Thomas. "Are you with them on this?"

Thomas looked unhappy. "I had hoped that you would have a better plan, sir."

"And you, Dr. Brooks?"

"Well—it seems feasible. I feel much as Thomas does."

"Graham?"

The man gave him answer by silence. Wilkie looked up and then away again.

"Mitsui?"

"I'll go back outside, sir. I have things to finish."

"Scheer?"

Scheer's jaw muscles quivered. "I'll stick if you do, sir."

"Thanks." He turned to the rest. "I said, 'No!' and I mean it. If any of you leave here, it will be in direct violation of your oaths. That goes for you, Thomas! I'm not being arbitrary about this. The thing you propose to do is on all fours with the raid I canceled. So long as the people of the United States are hostages at the mercy of the PanAsians we can not take direct military action! It doesn't make any difference whether the attack comes from inside or outside, thousands, maybe millions, of innocent people will pay for it with their lives!"

He was very much wrought up, but not too much

so to look around and see what effect his words were having. He had them back—or would have them in a few minutes. All but Calhoun. They were looking disturbed.

"Supposing you are right, sir"—it was Brooks speaking very gravely—"supposing you are right, is there anything we *can* do?"

"I explained that once before. We have to form what I called a 'sixth column,' lie low, study out their weak points, and work on them."

"I see. Perhaps you are right. Perhaps it is necessary. But it calls for a sort of patience more suited to gods than to men."

He almost had it then. What was it?

"So 'There'll be pie in the sky by and by,' " quoted Calhoun. "You should have been a preacher, Major Ardmore. We prefer action."

That was it! That was it!

"You're almost right," Ardmore answered. "Have you listened to Thomas' report?"

"I listened to the play-back."

"Do you recall the one respect in which white men are still permitted to organize?"

"Why, no, I don't recall that there was one."

"None? Nowhere that they were permitted to assemble?"

"I know!" Thomas burst in. "Churches!"

Ardmore waited a moment for it to sink in, then he said very softly, "Has it ever occurred to any of you to think of the possibilities in *founding a new religion?*"

There was a short and startled silence. Calhoun broke it.

71

"The man's gone mad!"

"Take it easy, Colonel," Ardmore said mildly. "I don't blame you for thinking that I've gone crazy. It does sound crazy to talk about founding a new religion when what we want is military action against the PanAsians. But consider—what we need is an organization that can be trained and armed to fight. That and a communication system which will enable us to coordinate the whole activity. And we have to do the whole thing under the eyes of the PanAsians without arousing their suspicions. If we were a religious sect instead of a military organization, all that would be possible."

"It's preposterous! I'll have nothing to do with it."

"Please, Colonel. We need you badly. On that matter of a communication system now— Imagine temples in every city in the country hooking together with a communication system and the whole thing hooked in here at the Citadel."

Calhoun snorted. "Yes, and the Asiatics listening in to everything you say!"

"That's why we need you, Colonel. Couldn't you devise a system that they couldn't trap? Something like a radio, maybe, but operating in one of the additional spectra so that their instruments could not detect it? Or couldn't you?"

Calhoun snorted again but with a different intonation. "Why, certainly I could. The problem is elementary."

"That's exactly why we have to have you, Colonel—to solve problems that are elementary to a man of your genius"—Ardmore felt slightly nauseated inside: this was worse than writing advertising copy—

"but which are miracles for the rest of us. That's what a religion needs—miracles! You'll be called on to produce effects that will strain even your genius, things that the PanAsians cannot possibly understand, and will think supernatural." Seeing Calhoun still hesitate, he added, "You can do it, can't you?"

"Certainly, I can, my dear Major."

"Fine. How soon can you let me have a communication method which can't be compromised or detected?"

"Impossible to say, but it won't take long. I still don't see the sense to your scheme, Major, but I will turn my attention to the research you say you require." He got up and went out, a procession of one.

"Major?" Wilkie asked for attention.

"What? Oh, yes, Wilkie."

"I can design such a communication system for you."

"I don't doubt it a damn bit, but we are going to need all the talent we can stir up for this job. There will be plenty for you to do, too. Now as to the rest of the scheme, here's what I have in mind—just a rough idea, and I want you all to kick it around as much as possible until we get it as nearly foolproof as possible.

"We'll go through all the motions of setting up an evangelical religion, and try to get people to come to our services. Once we get 'em in where we can talk to 'em, we can pick out the ones that can be trusted and enlist them in the army. We'll make them deacons, or something, in the church. Our big angle will be charity—you come in on that, Wilkie with the transmutation process. You will turn out a lot of precious metal, gold mostly, so that we will have ready cash to work with. We feed the poor and the hungry—the PanAsians have provided us with plenty of those!—and pretty soon we'll have 'em coming to us in droves.

"But that isn't the half of it. We really will go in for miracles in a big way. Not only to impress the white population—that's secondary—but to confuse our lords and masters. We'll do things they can't understand, make them uneasy, uncertain of themselves. Never anything against them, you understand. We'll be loyal subjects of the Empire in every possible way, but we'll be able to do things that they can't. That will upset them and make them nervous." It was taking shape in his mind like a well-thought-out advertising campaign. "By the time we are ready to strike in force, we should have them demoralized, afraid of us, half hysterical."

They were beginning to be infected with some of his enthusiasm; but the scheme was conceived from a viewpoint more or less foreign to their habits of thought. "Maybe this will work, Chief," objected Thomas, "I don't say that it won't, but how do you propose to get it underway? Won't the Asiatic administrators smell a rat in the sudden appearance of a new religion?"

"Maybe so, but I don't think it likely. All Western religions look equally screwy to them. They know we have dozens of religions and they don't know anything about most of them. That's one respect in which the Era of Nonintercourse will be useful to us. They don't know much about our institutions since the Nonintercourse Act. This will just look like

74

any one of half a dozen cockeyed cults of the sort that spring up overnight in Southern California."

"But about that springing-up business, Chief— How do we start out? We can't just walk out of the Citadel, buttonhole one of the yellow boys, and say, 'I'm John the Baptist.' "

"No, we can't. That's a point that has to be worked out. Has anybody any ideas?"

The silence that followed was thick with intense concentration. Finally Graham proposed, "Why not just set up in business, and wait to be noticed?"

"How do you mean?"

"Well, we've got enough people right here to operate on a small scale. If we had a temple somewhere, one of us could be the priest, and the others could be disciples or something. Then just wait to be noticed."

"H-m-m-m. You've got something there, Graham. But we'll open up on the biggest scale we can manage. We'll all be priests and altar attendants and so forth, and I'll send Thomas out to stir up a congregation for us among his pals. No, wait. Let 'em come in as pilgrims. We'll start this off with a whispering campaign among the hobos, send it over the grapevine. We'll have 'em say, 'The Disciple is coming!' "

"What does that mean?" Scheer inquired.

"Nothing, yet. But it will, when the time comes. Now look— Graham, you're an artist. You're going to have to get dinner with your left hand for a few days. Your right will be busy sketching out ideas for robes and altars and props in general—sacerdotal stuff. I guess the interior and exterior of the temple will be mostly up to you, too."

"Where will the temple be located?"

"Well, now, that's a question. It shouldn't be too far from here unless we abandon the Citadel entirely. That doesn't seem expedient; we need it for a base and a laboratory. But the temple can't be too close, for we can't afford to attract special attention to this mountainside." Ardmore drummed on the table. "It's a difficult matter."

"Why not," offered Dr. Brooks, "make this the temple?"

"Huh?"

"I don't mean this room, of course, but why not put the first temple right on top of the Citadel? It would be very convenient."

"So it would, doctor, but it would certainly draw a lot of unhealthy attention to— Wait a minute! I think I see what you mean." He turned to Wilkie. "Bob, how could you use the Ledbetter effect to conceal the existence of the Citadel, if the Mother Temple sat right on top of it? Could it be done?"

Wilkie looked more puzzled and collie-doggish than ever. "The Ledbetter effect wouldn't do it. Do you especially want to use the Ledbetter effect? Because if you don't it wouldn't be hard to rig a type-seven screen in the magneto-gravitic spectrum so that electromagnetic type instruments would be completely blanked out. You see—"

"Of course I don't care what you use! I don't even know the names of the stuff you laboratory boys use—all I want is the results. O.K.—you take care of that. We'll completely design the temple here, get all the materials laid out and ready to assemble down below, then break through to the surface and run the thing up as fast as possible. Anyone have any idea how long that will take? I'm afraid my own experience doesn't run to building construction."

Wilkie and Scheer engaged in a whispered consultation. Presently Wilkie broke off and said, "Don't worry too much about that, Chief. It will be a power job."

"What sort?"

"You've got a memorandum on your desk about the stuff. The traction and pressure control we developed from the earlier Ledbetter experiments."

"Yes, Major," Scheer added, "you can forget it; I'll take care of the job. With tractors and pressors in an aggravitic field, it won't take any longer than assembling a cardboard model. Matter of fact, I'll practice on a cardboard model before we run up the main job."

"O.K., troops," Ardmore smilingly agreed, with the lightheartedness that comes from the prospect of plenty of hard work, "that's the way I like to hear you talk. The powwow is adjourned for now. Get going! Thomas, come with me."

"Just a second, Chief," Brooks added as he got up to follow him, "couldn't we—" They went out the door, still talking.

Despite Scheer's optimism the task of building a temple on the mountain top above the Citadel developed unexpected headaches. None of the little band had had any real experience with large construction jobs. Ardmore, Graham, and Thomas knew nothing at all of such things, although Thomas had done plenty of work with his hands, some of it carpentry. Calhoun was a mathematician and by temperament undisposed to trouble himself with such menial pursuits in any case. Brooks was willing enough but he was a biologist, not an engineer. Wilkie was a brilliant physicist and, along lines related to his specialty, a competent engineer; he could design a piece of new apparatus necessary to his work quite handily.

However, Wilkie had built no bridges, designed no dams, bossed no gangs of sweating men. Nevertheless the job devolved on him by Hobson's choice. Scheer was not competent to build a large building; he thought that he was, but he thought in terms of small things, tools, patterns, and other items that fitted into a machine shop. He could build a scale model of a large building, but he simply did not understand heavy construction.

It was up to Wilkie.

He showed up in Ardmore's office a few days later with a roll of drawings under his arm. "Uh, Chief?"

"Eh? Oh, come in, Bob. Sit down. What's eating on you? When do we start building the temple? See here—I've been thinking about other ways to conceal the fact that the Citadel will be under the temple. Do you suppose you could arrange the altar so that—"

"Excuse me, Chief."

"Eh?"

"We can incorporate most any dodge you want into the design, but I've got to know something more about the design first."

"That's your problem—yours and Graham's."

"Yes, sir. But how big do you want it to be?"

"How big? Oh, I don't know, exactly. It has to be *big*." Ardmore made a sweeping motion with both hands that took in floor, walls, and ceiling. "It has to be impressive."

"How about thirty feet in the largest dimension?"

"Thirty feet? Why, that's ridiculous! You aren't building a soft-drinks stand; you're building the mother temple of a great religion—of course you aren't, but you've got to think of it that way. It's got to knock their eyes out. What's the trouble? Materials?"

Wilkie shook his head. "No, with Ledbetter-type transmutation materials are not a problem. We can use the mountain itself for materials."

"That's what I thought you intended to do. Carve out big chunks of granite and use your tractor and pressor beams to lay them up like giant bricks."

"Oh, no!"

"No? Why not?"

"Well, we could, but when we got through it wouldn't look like much—and I don't know how we would roof it over. What I intended to do was to use the Ledbetter effect not just for cutting or quarrying, but to make—transmute—the materials I want. You see, granite is principally oxides of silicon. That complicates things a little because both elements are fairly near the lower end of the periodic table. Unless we go to a lot of trouble and get rid of a lot of excess energy—a tremendous amount; darn near as much as the Memphis power pile develops—as I say, unless we arrange to bleed off all that power, and right now I don't see just how we could do it, then—"

"Get to the point, man!"

"I was getting to the point, sir," Wilkie answered in hurt tones. "Transmutations from the top or the bottom of the periodic scale toward the middle give off power; contrariwise, they absorb energy. Way back in the middle of the last century they found out how to do the first sort; that's what atom bombs are based on. But to handle transmutations for building materials, you don't want to give off energy like an atom bomb or a power pile. It would be embarrassing."

"I should think so!"

"So I'll use the second sort, the energy-absorbing sort. As a matter of fact I'll balance them. Take magnesium for instance. It lies between silicon and oxygen. The binding energies involved—"

"Wilkie!"

"Yes, sir?"

"Just assume that I never got through third grade. Now can you make the materials you need, or can't you?"

"Oh, yes, sir, I can make them."

"Then how can I be of help to you?"

"Well, sir, it's the matter of putting the roof on— and the size. You say a thirty-foot over-all dimension is no good—"

"No good at all. Did you see the North American Exposition? Remember the General Atomics Exhibit?"

"I've seen pictures of it."

"I want something as gaudy and impressive as that, only bigger. Now why are you limited to thirty feet?"

"Well, sir, a panel six by thirty is the biggest I can

squeeze out through the door, allowing for the turn in the passage."

"Take 'em up through the scout-car lift."

"I thought of that. It will take a panel thirteen feet wide, which is good, but the maximum length is then only twenty-seven feet. There's a corner to turn between the hangar and the lift."

"Hmm— Look, can you weld with that magic gimmick? I thought you could build the temple in sections, down below here, then assemble it above ground?"

"That was the idea. Yes, I suppose we could weld walls as big as you want. But look, major, how big a building do you want?"

"As big as you can manage."

"But how big do you *want?*"

Ardmore told him. Wilkie whistled. "I suppose it's possible to give you walls that big, but I don't see any way to roof it over."

"Seems to me I've seen buildings with that much clear span."

"Yes, of course. You give me the services of construction engineers and architects and heavy industry to build the trusses needed to take that span and I'll build you as big a temple as you want. But Scheer and I can't do it alone, even with pressors and tractors to do all the heavy work. I'm sorry, sir, but I don't see an answer."

Ardmore stood up and put a hand on Wilkie's arm. "You mean you don't see an answer yet. Don't get upset, Bob. I'll take whatever you build. But just remember— This is going to be our first public display. A lot depends on it. We can't expect to make

much impression on our overlords with a hotdog
stand. Make it as big as you can. I'd like something
about as impressive as the Great Pyramid—but don't
take that long to build it."

Wilkie looked worried. "I'll try, sir. I'll go back
and think about it."

"Fine!"

When Wilkie had gone Ardmore turned to Thomas.
"What do you think about it, Jeff? Am I asking too
much?"

"I was just wondering," Thomas said slowly, "why
you set so much store by this temple?"

"Well, in the first place it gives a perfect cover up
for the Citadel. If we are going to do anything more
than sit here and die of old age, the time will come
when a lot of people will have to be going in and out
of here. We can't keep the location secret under
those circumstances so we will have to have a reason,
a cover up. People are always going in and out of a
church building—worship and so forth. I want to
cover up the 'and so forth.' "

"I understand that. But a building with thirty-foot
maximum dimensions can cover up a secret stairway
quite as well as the sort of convention-hall job you
are asking young Wilkie to throw up."

Ardmore squirmed. Damn it—couldn't anyone but
himself see the value of advertising? "Look, Jeff, this
whole deal depends on making the right impression
at the start. If Columbus had come in asking for a
dime, he would have been thrown out of the palace
on his ear. As it was, he got the crown jewels. We've
got to have an impressive front."

"I suppose so," Thomas answered without conviction.

Several days later Wilkie asked permission for Scheer and himself to go outside. Finding that they did not intend to go far, Ardmore gave permission, after impressing on them the need for extreme caution.

He encountered them some time later proceeding down the main passage toward the laboratories. They had an enormous granite boulder. Scheer was supporting it clear of walls and floor by means of tractors and pressors generated by a portable Ledbetter projector strapped as a pack on his shoulders. Wilkie had tied a line around the great chunk of rock and was leading it as if it were a cow. "Great Scott!" said Ardmore. "What y' got there?"

"Uh, a piece of mountain, sir."

"So I see. But why?"

Wilkie looked mysterious. "Major, could you spare some time later in the day? We might have something to show you."

"If you won't talk, you won't talk. Very well."

Wilkie phoned him later, much later, asked him to come and suggested that Thomas come, too. When they arrived in the designated shop room everyone was present except Calhoun. Wilkie greeted them and said, "With your permission, we'll start, Major."

"Don't be so formal. Aren't you going to wait for Colonel Calhoun?"

"I invited him, but he declined."

"Go ahead then."

"Yes, sir." Wilkie turned to the rest. "This piece of granite represents the mountain top above us. Go ahead, Scheer."

Wilkie took position at a Ledbetter projector. Scheer was already at one; it had been specially fitted with sights and some other gadgetry that Ardmore could not identify. Scheer pressed a couple of studs; a pencil beam of light sprang out.

Using it as if it were a saw he sliced the top off the boulder. Wilkie caught the separated portion with a tractor-pressor combination and moved it aside. He set his controls and it hung in air; where it had been the stone was flat and of mirror polish. "That's the temple's base," said Wilkie.

Scheer continued carving with his pencil beam, trucking his projector around as necessary. The flat top had now been squared off; the square was the summit of a four-sided truncated pyramid. That done, he started carving steps down one side of the figure. "That's enough, Scheer," Wilkie commanded. "Let's make a wall. Prepare the surface."

Scheer did something with his projector. No beam could be seen, but the flat upper surface turned black. "Carbon," announced Wilkie. "Industrial diamonds probably. That's our work bench. O.K., Scheer." Wilkie moved the detached chunk back over the "bench"; Scheer carved off a piece; it turned molten, dripped down on the flat surface, spread to the edges and stopped. It now had a white metallic sheen. As it cooled Scheer nipped each corner, then, using one pressor as a vise to hold it firmly to the boulder and another as a moving wedge, he turned each corner up. It was now a shallow, open box, two feet square and an inch deep. Wilkie whisked it aside and hung it in air.

The process was repeated, but this time a single

sheet rather than a box was formed. Wilkie put it out of the way and put the box back on the pedestal. "Let's stuff the turkey," announced Wilkie.

He transferred the chopped-off chunk back to a position over the open box. Scheer carved off a piece and lowered it into the box, then played a beam on it. It melted down and spread over the bottom. "Granite is practically glass," lectured Wilkie, "and what we want is foamed glass, so we use no transmutation in this step—except the least, little bit to make the gases to foam it. Let's have a shot of nitrogen, Scheer." The master sergeant nodded and irradiated the mess for a split second; it foamed up like boiling fudge, filling the shallow box to the rim, and froze.

Wilkie snagged the simple sheet out of the air and caused it to hover over the filled box, then to settle so that it lay, somewhat unevenly, as a cover. "Iron it down, Scheer."

The sheet glowed red and settled in place, pressed flat by an invisible hand. Scheer walked his projector around, welding the cover of the box to the box proper. When he had finished Wilkie set the filled box up on edge at one edge of the pedestal. Leaving the controls of his projector set to hold it there, he walked over to the far side of the room where a tarpaulin covered a pile of something on a bench.

"To save your time and for practice we made four others earlier," he explained and whipped off the tarpaulin. Disclosed were a stack of sandwich panels exactly like that one just created. He did not touch them; instead Scheer lifted them off by projector one at a time and built a cube, using the newly made panel as the first face and the pedestal as the bottom of the cube. Wilkie returned to his projector and held the structure rigid while Scheer welded each seam. "Scheer is much more accurate than I am," he explained. "I give him all the tough parts. O.K., Scheer—how about a door?"

"How big?" grunted the sergeant, speaking for the first time.

"Use your judgment. Eight inches high would be all right."

Scheer grunted again and carved a rectangular opening in the side facing the slope on which he had begun earlier to carve steps. When he finished Wilkie announced, "There's your temple, boss."

No human hand had touched the boulder nor anything made from it, from start to finish.

The applause sounded like considerably more than five people. Wilkie turned pink; Scheer worked his jaw muscles. They crowded around it. "Is it 'hot'?" inquired Brooks.

"No," answered Mitsui. "I touched it."

"I didn't mean that."

"No, it's not 'hot'," Wilkie reassured him, "not with the Ledbetter process. Stable isotopes, all of them."

Ardmore straightened up from a close inspection. "I take it you intend to do the whole thing outdoors?"

"Is that all right, Major? Of course we could work down below and assemble it up above, from small panels—but I'm sure that would take just as long as to work from scratch with big panels. And I'm not sure about assembling the roof from small units. Sandwich panels like these are the lightest, strongest, stiffest structure we can use. It was the problem of that big roof span you want that caused us to work out this system."

"Do it your way. I'm sure you know what you're doing."

"Of course," admitted Wilkie, "we can't *finish* it in this short a time. This is just the shell. I don't know how long it will take to dress it up."

"Dress it up?" inquired Graham. "When you've got a fine, great simple shape why belittle it with decoration? The cube is one of the purest and most beautiful shapes possible."

"I agree with Graham," Ardmore commented. "That's your temple, right there. Nothing makes a more effective display than great, unbroken masses. When you've got something simple and effective, don't louse it up."

Wilkie shrugged. "I wouldn't know. I thought you wanted something fancy."

"This *is* fancy. But see here, Bob, one thing puzzles me. Mind you, I'm not criticizing—I'd as soon think of criticizing the Days of Creation—but tell me this: why did you take a chance on going outside? Why didn't you just go into one of the unoccupied rooms, peel off the wall coating and use that magic knife to carve a chunk of granite right out of the heart of the mountain?"

Wilkie looked thunderstruck. "I never thought of that."

CHAPTER FIVE

A PATROL HELICOPTER CRUISED SLOWLY SOUTH FROM Denver. The PanAsian lieutenant commanding it consulted a recently constructed aerial mosaic map and indicated to the pilot that he was to hover. Yes, there it was, a *great cubical building rising from the shoulder of a mountain*. It had been picked up by the cartographical survey of the Heavenly Emperor's new Western Realm and he had been sent to investigate.

The lieutenant regarded the job as a simple routine matter. Although the building did not appear in the records of the administrative district in which it was located there was nothing surprising in that. The newly conquered territory was enormous in extent, the aborigines, with their loose undisciplined ways—so characteristic of all the inferior races—kept no proper records of anything. It might be years before everything in this wild new country was properly indexed and cross-filed, particularly as this pale anemic people was almost childishly resistant to the benefits of civilization.

Yes, it would be a long job, perhaps longer than the Amalgamation of India. He sighed to himself. He had received a letter that morning from his principal wife informing him that his second wife had presented him with a man-child. Should he request that he be reclassified as a permanent colonist in order that his family might join him here, or should he pray for leave, long overdue?

Those were no thoughts for a man on the Heavenly Emperor's duty! He recited over to himself the Seven Principles of the Warrior Race and indicated to the pilot an alp in which to land.

The building was more impressive from the ground, a great square featureless mass, fully two hundred yards across in every dimension. The face toward him shone with a clear monochromatic emerald green, although it faced away from the afternoon sun. He could see a little of the wall to the right; it was golden.

His task group of one squad filed out of the helicopter after him and were followed by the mountain guide who had been impressed for this service. He spoke to the white man in English. "Have you seen this building before?"

"No, Master."

"Why not?"

"This part of the mountains is new to me."

The man was probably lying, but it was useless to punish him. He dropped the matter. "Lead on."

They trudged steadily up the slope toward the immense cube to where a broad flight of steps, wider still than the cube itself, led to its nearer face. The lieutenant hesitated momentarily before starting to mount them. He was aware of a general feeling of unease, a sense of mild disquietude, as if a voice were warning him of unnamed danger.

He set foot on the first step. A single deep clear note rolled across the canyon; the feeling of uneasiness swelled to an irrational dread. He could see that his men were infected with it. Resolutely he mounted the second step. Another and different tone echoed through the hills.

He marched steadily up the long flight, his men following reluctantly. A slow, ponderous and infinitely tragic largo kept time to his labored steps—labored, because the treads were just too broad and the lifts just too high for comfort. The feeling of impending disaster, of inescapable doom, grew steadily greater as he approached the building.

Two doors of heroic size swung slowly open as the lieutenant ascended. In the archway thus created stood a human figure, a man, dressed in emerald robes that brushed the floor. White hair and flowing beard framed a face of benign dignity. He moved majestically forward from the doorway, reaching the top of the flight of steps just as the lieutenant attained it. The lieutenant noted with amazement that a halo flickered unsubstantially around the old man's head. But he had little time to consider it; the old man raised his right hand in benediction and spoke:

"Peace be unto you!"

And it was *so!* The feeling of dread, of irrational fright, dropped away from the PanAsian as if someone had turned a switch. In his relief he found himself regarding this member of an inferior race—so evidently a priest—with a warmth reserved for equals. He recalled the Admonitions for dealing with inferior religions.

"What is this place, Holy One?"

"You stand at the threshold of the Temple of Mota, Lord of Lords and Lord of All!"

"Mota—h-m-m-m." He could not recall such a god, but it did not matter. These sallow creatures had a thousand strange gods. Three things only do slaves require, food, work, and their gods, and of the three their gods must never be touched, else they grow troublesome. So said the Precepts for Ruling. "Who are you?"

"I am an humble priest, First Server of Shaam, Lord of Peace."

"Shaam? I thought you said Mota was your god?"

"We serve the Lord Mota in six of his thousand attributes. You serve him in your way. Even the Heavenly Emperor serves him in his. My duty is to the Lord of Peace."

This was perilously close to treason, the lieutenant thought, if not to blasphemy. Still, it may be that the gods have many names, and the native did not seem disposed to make trouble. "Very well, old Holy One, the Heavenly Emperor permits you to serve your god as you see him, but I must inspect for the Empire. Stand aside."

The old man did not move, but answered regretfully, "I am sorry, Master. It cannot be."

"It must be. Stand aside!"

"Please, Master, I beg of you! It is not possible for you to enter here. In these attributes Mota is Lord of the white men. You must go to your own temple; you cannot enter this one. It is death to any but his followers."

"You threaten me?"

"No, Master, no—we serve the Emperor, as our faith requires. But this thing the Lord Mota Himself forbids. I cannot save you if you offend."

"On the Heavenly Emperor's service—stand aside!" He strode steadily across the broad terrace toward the door, his squad clomping stolidly after him. The panic dread clutched at him as he marched and increased in intensity as he approached the great door. His heart seemed constricted, and a mad longing to flee clamored through him senselessly. Only the fatalistic courage of his training made him go on. Through the door he saw a vast empty hall and on the far side an altar, large in itself, but dwarfed by the mammoth proportions of the room. The inner walls shone, each with its own light, red, blue, green, golden. The ceiling was a perfect, flawless white, the floor an equally perfect black.

There was nothing to be afraid of here, he told himself, this illogical but horribly real dread was a sickness, unworthy of a warrior. He stepped across the threshold. A momentary dizziness, a flash of terrifying insecurity and he collapsed.

His squad, close at his heels, had no more warning.

Ardmore came trotting out of concealment. "Nice work, Jeff," he called out, "you should be on the stage!"

The old priest relaxed. "Thanks, Chief. What happens next?"

"We'll have time to figure that out." He turned toward the altar and shouted, "Scheer!"

"Yes, sir!"

"Turn off the fourteen-cycle note!" He added to Thomas, "Those damned subsonics give me the creeping horrors even when I know what's going on. I wonder what effect it had on our pal here?"

"He was cracking up, I believe. I never thought he'd make it to the doorway."

"I don't blame him. It made me want to howl like a dog, and *I* ordered it turned on. There's nothing like the fear of something you can't understand to break a man down. Well, we got a bear by the tail. Now to figure out a way to turn loose—"

"How about *him?*" Thomas jerked his head toward the mountaineer, who still stood near the head of the great flight of steps.

"Oh, yes." Ardmore whistled at him and shouted, "Hey you—come here!"

The man hesitated, and Ardmore added, "Damn it—we're white men! Can't you see that?"

The man answered, "I see it, but I don't like it." Nevertheless he slowly approached.

Ardmore said, "This is a piece of razzle-dazzle for the benefit of our yellow brethren. Now that you're in it, you're in it! Are you game?"

The other members of the personnel of the Citadel had gathered around by this time. The mountain guide glanced around at their faces. "It doesn't look as if I had much choice."

"Maybe not, but we would rather have a volunteer than a prisoner."

The mountaineer shifted tobacco from left cheek to right, glanced around the immaculate pavement for a place to spit, decided not to, and answered. "What's the game?"

"It's a frame-up on our Asiatic bosses. We plan to give them the run-around—with the help of God and the great Lord Mota."

The guide looked them over again, then suddenly stuck out his hand and said, "I'm in."

"Fine," agreed Ardmore, taking his hand. "What's your name?"

"Howe. Alexander Hamilton Howe. Friends call me Alec."

"O.K., Alec. Now what can you do? Can you cook?" he added.

"Some."

"Good." He turned away. "Graham, he's your man for now. I'll talk with him later. Now—Jeff, did it seem to you that one of those monkeys went down a little slowly?"

"Maybe. Why?"

"This one; wasn't it?" He touched one of the quiet, sprawled figures with his shoe.

"I think so."

"All right, I want to check up on him before we bring them to. If he's a Mongolian he should have keeled over quicker. Dr. Brooks, will you give this laddie's reflexes a work-out? And don't be too gentle about it."

Brooks managed to produce some jerks in short order. Seeing this, Ardmore reached down and set his thumb firmly on the exposed nerve under the ear. The soldier came to his knees, writhing. "All right, bud—explain yourself." The soldier stared impassively. Ardmore studied his face for a moment, then made a quick gesture, which was protected from the gaze of the others by his body.

"Why didn't you say so?" asked the PanAsian soldier.

"I must say it's a good make-up job," commented Ardmore admiringly. "What's your name and rank?"

"Tattoo and plastic surgery," the other returned. "Name's Downer, captain, United States army."

"Mine's Ardmore. Major Ardmore."

"Glad to know you, Major." They shook hands. "Very glad, I should say. I've been hanging on for months, wondering who to report to and how."

"Well, we can certainly use you. It's a scratch organization. I've got to get busy now—we'll talk later." He turned away. "Places, gentlemen. Second act. Check each other's make-up. Wilkie, see to it that Howe and Downer are out of sight. We are going to bring our drowsy guests back to consciousness."

They started to comply. Downer touched Ardmore's sleeve.

"Just a moment, Major. I don't know your layout, but before we go any further, are you sure you don't want me to stay on my present assignment?"

"Eh? H-m-m-m—you've got something there. Are you willing to do it?"

"I'm willing to do it, if it's useful," Downer replied soberly.

"It would be useful. Thomas, come here." The

three of them went into a short conference and arranged a way for Downer to report through the grapevine, and Ardmore told him as much about the set-up as he needed to know. "Well, good luck, old man," he concluded. "Get back down there and play dead, and we'll reanimate your messmates."

Thomas, Ardmore, and Calhoun attended the Asiatic lieutenant as his eyes flickered open. "Praise be!" intoned Thomas. "The Master lives!"

The lieutenant stared around him, shook his head, then reached for his sidearm. Ardmore, impressive in the red robes of Dis, Lord of Destruction, held up a hand. "Careful, Master, please! I have beseeched my Lord Dis to return you to us. Do not offend him again."

The Asiatic hesitated, then asked, "What happened?"

"The Lord Mota, acting through Dis, the Destroyer, took you for his own. We prayed and wept and beseeched Tamar, Lady of Mercy, to intercede for us." He swept an arm toward the open door. Wilkie, Graham, and Brooks, appropriately clad, were still busily genuflecting before the altar. "Graciously, our prayer was answered. Go in peace!"

Scheer, at the control board, picked this moment to increase the volume on the fourteen-cycle note. With nameless fear pressing his heart, confused, baffled, the lieutenant took the easy way out. He gathered his men about him and marched back down the broad flight of stairs, colossal organ music still following him in awful, inescapable accompaniment.

"Well, that's that," Ardmore commented as the little group disappeared in the distance. "First round to God's chilluns. Thomas, I want you to start into town at once."

"So?"

"In your robes and full paraphernalia. Seek out the district boss and register formal complaint that Lieutenant Stinkyface did wrongfully profane our sacred places to the great indignation of our gods, and pray for assurance that it will not happen again. You want to be on your high horse about the whole matter— righteous indignation, you know—but, oh, very respectful to temporal authority."

"I appreciate the confidence you place in me," Thomas said with sardonic grimness. Ardmore grinned at him.

"I know it's a tough assignment, fella, but a lot depends on it. If we can make use of their own customs and rules to establish a precedent right now which sets us up as a legitimate religion, entitled to all the usual immunites, we've got half the battle won."

"Suppose they ask for my identification card?"

"If you carry yourself with sufficient arrogance they will never get around to asking for it. Just think about the typical clubwoman and try to show that much bulge. I want 'em to get used to the idea that anyone with the staff and the robes and the halo carries his identification just in his appearance. It will save us trouble later."

"I'll try—but I'm not promising anything."

"I think you can do it. Anyhow, you are going out equipped with enough stuff to keep you safe. Keep your shield turned on whenever you are around any of 'em. Don't try to account for it in any way; just let 'em bounce off it, if they close in on you. It's a miracle—no need to explain."

"O.K."

The lieutenant's report was not satisfactory to his superiors. As for that, it was not satisfactory to himself. He felt an acute sense of loss of personal honor, of face, which the words of his immediate superior did nothing to lessen. "You, an officer in the army of the Heavenly Emperor, have permitted yourself to look small in the eyes of a subject race. What have you to say?"

"Your forgiveness, sire!"

"Not for me—it is a matter for you to settle with your ancestors."

"I hear, sire!" He caressed the short sword which hung at his side.

"Let there be no haste; I intend for you to tell your tale in person to the Imperial Hand."

The local Hand of the Emperor, military governor of that region which included Denver and the Citadel, was no more pleased than his junior. "What possessed you to enter their holy place? These people are childlike, excitable. Your action could be the regrettable cause of assassinations of many more valuable than yourself. We cannot be forever wasting slaves to teach them lessons."

"I am unworthy, sire."

"I do not dispute that. You may go." The lieutenant departed, to join, not his family, but his ancestors.

The Imperial Hand turned to his adjutant. "We will probably be petitioned by this cult. See that the petitioners are pacified and assured that their gods will not be disturbed. Note the characteristics of the sect and send out a general warning to deal gently with it." He sighed. "These savages and their false gods! I grow weary of them. Yet they are necessary; the priests and the gods of slaves always fight on the side of the Masters. It is a rule of nature."

"You have spoken, sire."

Ardmore was glad to see Thomas return to the Citadel. In spite of his confidence in Jeff's ability to handle himself in a tight place, in spite of the assurance that Calhoun had given him that the protective shield, properly handled, would protect the wearer from anything that the PanAsian could bring on it, he had been in a state of nerves ever since Thomas had set out to register a complaint with the Asiatic authorities. After all, the attitude of the PanAsians toward local religions might be one of bare toleration rather than special encouragement.

"Welcome home, old boy!" he shouted, pounding him on the back. "I'm glad to see your ugly face— tell me what happened?"

"Give me time to get out of this bloody bathrobe, and I'll tell you. Got a cigarette? That's a bad point about being a holy man; they don't smoke."

"Sure. Here. Had anything to eat?"

"Not recently."

Ardmore flipped the intercommunicator to Kitchen. "Alec, rustle up some groceries for Lieutenant Thomas. And tell the troops they can hear his story if they come around to my office."

"Ask him if he has any avocados."

Ardmore did so. "He says they're still in quick-freeze, but he'll thaw one out. Now let's have your story. What did Little Red Riding Hood say to the wolf?"

"Well—you'll hardly believe it, Chief, but I didn't have any trouble at all. When I got into town, I marched right straight up to the first PanAsian policeman I found, stepped off the curb, and struck the old benediction pose—staff in my left hand, right hand pawing the air; none of this handsfolded and head down stuff that white men are supposed to use. Then I said, 'Peace be unto you! Will the Master direct his servant to the seat of the Heavenly Emperor's government?'

"I don't think he understood much English. He seemed startled at my manner, and got hold of another flatface to help him. This one knew more English and I repeated my request. They palavered in that damned singsong tongue of theirs, then conducted me to the palace of the Emperor's Hand. We made quite a procession—one on each side and me walking fast so that I kept about even or a little in front of them."

"Good advertising," Ardmore approved.

"That's what I thought. Anyway, they got me there and I told my story to some underofficial. The results astounded me. I was whisked right straight up to the Hand himself."

"The hell you say!"

"Wait a minute—here's the pay-off. I'll admit I was scared, but I said to myself 'Jeff, old boy, if you start to crawl now, you'll never get out of here alive.' I knew a white man is expected to drop to his knees before an official of that rank. I didn't; I gave him the same standing benediction I had given his flunkies. And he let me get away with it! He looked me over and said, 'I thank you for your blessing, Holy One. You may approach.' He speaks excellent English, by the way.

"Well, I gave him a reasonably accurate version of what happened here—the official version, you understand—and he asked me a few questions."

"What sort of questions?"

"In the first place he wanted to know if my religion recognized the authority of the Emperor. I assured him that it did, that our followers were absolutely bound to obey temporal authority in all temporal matters, but that our creed commanded us to worship the true gods in our own fashion. Then I gave him a long theological spiel. I told him that all men worshipped God, but that God had a thousand attributes, each one a mystery. God in his wisdom had seen fit to appear to different races in different attributes *because it was not seemly for servant and master to worship in the same fashion*. Because of that, the six attributes of Mota, of Shaam, of Mens, of Tamar, of Barmac, and of Dis had been set aside for the white men, just as the Heavenly Emperor was an attribute reserved for the race of Master."

"How did he take it?"

"I gathered that he thought it was very sound doctrine—for slaves. He asked me what my church did besides holding services, and I told him that our principal desire is to minister to the poor and sick. He seemed pleased at that. I have an impression that our gracious overlords are finding relief a very serious problem."

"Relief? Do they give any relief?"

"Not exactly. But if you load prisoners into concentration camps you have to feed them something. The internal economy has largely broken down and they haven't got it straightened out yet. I think they would welcome a movement which would relieve them from worrying too much over how to feed the slaves."

"H-m-m-m. Anything else?"

"Nothing much. I assured him again that we, as spiritual leaders, were forbidden by our doctrines to have anything to do with politics, and he told me that we would not be molested in the future. Then he dismissed me. I repeated my benediction, turned my back on him, and stomped out."

"It seems to me," said Ardmore, "that you pretty thoroughly sold him a bill of goods."

"I wouldn't be too sure, Chief. That old scoundrel is shrewd and Machiavellian. I shouldn't call him a scoundrel, because he's not—by his standards. He's a statesman. I've got to admit he impressed me. Look—these PanAsians can't be stupid; they've conquered and held half a world, hundreds of millions of people. If they tolerate local religions, it's because they have found it to be smart politics. We've got to keep them thinking so in our case, in the face of smart and experienced administrators."

"No doubt you're right. We certainly must be careful not to underestimate them."

"I hadn't quite finished. Another escort picked me up on the way out of the palace and stayed with me. I walked along, paying no attention to them. My route out of town took me through the central market. There were hundreds of whites there, lined up in queues, waiting for a chance to buy food on their ration cards. I got an idea and decided to find out just how far my immunity extended. I stopped and climbed up on a box and started to preach to them."

Ardmore whistled. "Cripes, Jeff, you shouldn't have taken a chance like that!"

"But, Major, we needed to know, and I was fairly certain that the worst that could happen would be that they would make me stop."

"Well . . . yes, I suppose so. Anyhow the job requires that we take chances and you have to use your own judgment. Boldness may be the safest policy. Sorry I spoke—what happened?"

"My escort seemed dumbfounded at first, and not certain what to do. I went right ahead, watching them out of the corner of my eye. Pretty soon they were joined by a chappie who seemed to be senior to them. They held a confab, and the senior cop went away. He came back in about five minutes, and just stood there, watching me. I gathered that he had phoned in and had received instructions to let me alone."

"How did the crowd take it?"

"I think they were most impressed by the apparent fact that a white man was breaking one of the rules of the overlords and getting away with it. I didn't try to tell them much. I took as my text, 'The Disciple is coming!' and embroidered it with a lot of glittering generalities. I told them to be good boys and girls and not to be afraid, for the Disciple was coming to feed the hungry and heal the sick and console the bereaved."

"H-m-m-m. Now that you've started making promises, we had better get set to deliver."

"I was coming to that. Chief, I think that we had better set up a branch church in Denver right away."

"We've hardly got the personnel yet to start branching out."

"Are you sure? I don't like to set my opinion up against yours, but I don't see how we can gain many recruits unless we go where the recruits are. They're all set for it now; you may be sure that every white man in Denver is talking about the old beezer in the halo—in a *halo*, mind you!—who preached in the market place and the Asiatics didn't dare stop him. We'll pack 'em in!"

"Well . . . maybe you're right—"

"I think I am. Admitting that you can't spare the regular personnel from the Citadel, here's how we can work it; I'll go down to the city with Alec, locate a building that we can turn into a temple and start holding services. We can get along with the power units in the staffs at first, and Scheer can follow along and rebuild the interior of the temple and set up a proper unit in the altar. Once things are rolling I can turn the routine over to Alec. He'll be the local priest for Denver."

The others had drifted in one by one while Ardmore and Thomas were talking. Ardmore turned now to Alec Howe.

"How about it, Alec? Do you think you can make a noise like a priest, preach 'em sermons, organize charities, and that sort of thing?"

The mountain guide was slow to answer. "I think,

105

Major, that I would rather stay on the job I have now."

"It won't be so hard," Ardmore reassured him. "Thomas or I can write your sermons for you. The rest of it would consist largely in keeping your mouth shut and your eyes open, and in shooing likely prospects up here to be enlisted."

"It's not the sermons, Major. I can preach a sermon—I used to be a lay preacher in my youth. It's just that I can't reconcile this false religion with my conscience. I know you are working toward a worthy purpose and I've agreed to serve, but I'd rather stay in the kitchen."

Ardmore considered his words before replying. "Alec," he said at length, in a grave voice, "I think I can appreciate your viewpoint. I wouldn't want to ask any man to do anything against his own conscience. As a matter of fact, we would not have adopted the cloak of a religion had we seen any other practical way to fight for the United States. Does your faith forbid you to fight for your country?"

"No, it does not."

"Most of your work as a priest of this church would be to help the helpless. Doesn't that fit into your creed?"

"Naturally it does. That is exactly why I cannot do it in the name of a false God."

"But *is* it a false God? Do you believe that God cares very much what name you call Him as long as the work you perform is acceptable to Him? Now mind you," he added hastily, "I don't say that this so-called temple we have erected here is necessarily a House of the Lord, but isn't the worship of God a matter of how you feel in your heart rather than the verbal forms and the ceremonials used?"

"That's true, Major, every word you've said is gospel—but I just don't feel *right* about it."

Ardmore could see that Calhoun had been listening to this discussion with poorly concealed impatience. He decided to terminate it. "Alec, I want you to go now and think this over by yourself. Come see me tomorrow. If you can't reconcile this work to your conscience, I'll give you an unprejudiced discharge as a conscientious objector. It won't even be necessary for you to serve in the kitchen."

"I wouldn't want to go that far, Major. It seems to me—"

"No, really. If one is wrong, so is the other. I don't want to be responsible for requiring a man to do anything that might be a sin against his faith. Now you get along and think about it."

Ardmore hustled him out without giving him a chance to talk further.

Calhoun could contain himself no longer. "Well, really, Major, I must say! Is it your policy to compromise with superstition in the face of military necessity?"

"No, Colonel, it is not—but that superstition, as you call it, is in this case a military *fact*. Howe's case is the first example of something we are going to have to deal with—the attitude of the orthodox religions to the one we have trumped up."

"Maybe," suggested Wilkie, "we should have imitated the more usual religions."

"Perhaps. Perhaps. I thought of that, but somehow I couldn't see it. I can't picture one of us standing up and pretending to be a minister, say, of one of the regular protestant churches. I'm not much of a churchgoer, but I didn't think I could stomach it. Maybe when it comes right down to it, I'm bothered by the same thing that bothers Howe. But we've got to deal with it. We've got to consider the attitude of the other churches. We mustn't tread on their toes in any way we can help."

"Maybe this would help," Thomas suggested. "It could be one of the tenets of our church that we included and tolerated, even encouraged, any other form of worship that a man might favor. Besides that, every church, especially these days, has more social work than it can afford. We'll give the others financial assistance with no strings attached."

"Both of those things will help," Ardmore decided, "but it will be ticklish business. Whenever possible, we'll enlist the regular ministers and priests themselves. You can bet that every American will be for us, if he understands what we are aiming toward. The problem will be to decide which ones can be trusted with the whole secret. Now about Denver— Jeff, do you want to start back right away, tomorrow, maybe?"

"How about Howe?"

"He'll come around, I think."

"Just a moment, Major." It was Dr. Brooks, who had been sitting quietly, as usual, while the others talked. "I think it would be a good idea if we waited a day or two, until Scheer can make certain changes in the power units of the staffs."

"What sort of changes?"

"You will remember that we established experimentally that the Ledbetter effect could be used as a sterilizing agent?"

"Yes, of course."

"That is why we felt safe in predicting that we would help the sick. As a matter of fact we underestimated the potentialities of the method. I infected myself with anthrax earlier this week—"

"Anthrax! For God's sake, Doctor, what in the world do you mean by taking a chance like that?"

Brooks turned his mild eyes on Ardmore. "But it was obviously necessary," he explained patiently. "The guinea pig tests were positive, it is true, but human experimentation was necessary to establish the method. As I was saying, I infected myself with anthrax and permitted the disease to establish itself, then exposed myself to the Ledbetter effect in all wave lengths except that band of frequencies fatal to warm-blooded vertebrates. The disease disappeared. In less than an hour the natural balance of anabolism over catabolism had cleared up the residue of pathological symptoms. I was well."

"I'll be a cross-eyed intern! Do you think it will work on other diseases just as quickly?"

"I feel sure of it. Not only has such been the result with other diseases in the animal experimentation that I have conducted, but because of another unanticipated, though experimentally predictable, result. I've suffered from a rather severe cold in the head lately, as some of you may have noticed. The exposure not only cured the anthrax, it completely cleared up my cold. The cold virus involves a dozen or more known pathogenic organisms, and probably

109

as many more unknown ones. The exposure killed them all, indiscriminately."

"I'm delighted to get this report, Doctor," Ardmore answered. "In the long run this one development may be of more importance to the human race than any military use we may make of it now. But how does it affect the matter of establishing the branch church in Denver?"

"Well, sir, perhaps it doesn't. But I took the liberty of having Scheer modify one of the portable power units in order that healing might be conveniently carried on by any one of our agents even though equipped only with the staff. I thought you might prefer to wait until Scheer could add the same modification to the staffs designed to be used by Thomas and Howe."

"I think you are right, if it does not take too long. May I see the modification?"

Scheer demonstrated the staff he had worked over. Superficially it looked no different from the others. A six-foot rod was surmounted by a capital in the form of an ornate cube about four inches through. The faces of the cube were colored to correspond with the sides of the great temple. The base of the cube and the staff itself were covered with intricate designs in golden scroll-work, formal arabesques, and delicate bas-relief—all of which effectively concealed the controls of the power unit and projector located in the cubical capital.

Scheer had not changed the superficial appearance of the staff; he had simply added an additional circuit internally to the power unit in the cube which constrained it to oscillate only outside the band of frequencies fatal to vertebrate life. This circuit controlled the action of the power unit and projector whenever a certain leaf in the decorative design of the staff was pressed.

Scheer and Graham had labored together to create the staff's designing and redesigning to achieve an integrated whole in which mechanical action would be concealed in artistic camouflage. They made a good team. As a matter of fact their talents were not too far apart; the artist is two-thirds artisan and the artisan has essentially the same creative urge as the artist.

"I would suggest," added Brooks, when the new control had been explained and demonstrated, "that this new effect be attributed to Tamar, Lady of Mercy, and that her light be turned on when it is used."

"That's right. That's the idea," Ardmore approved. "Never use the staff for any purpose without turning on the color light associated with the particular god whose help you are supposed to be invoking. That's an invariable rule. Let 'em break their hearts trying to figure out how a simple monochromatic light can perform miracles."

"Why bother with the rigamarole?" inquired Calhoun. "The PanAsians can't possibly detect the effects we use in any case."

"There is a double reason, Colonel. By giving them a false lead to follow we hope to insure that they will bend their scientific efforts in the wrong direction. We can't afford to underestimate their ability. But even more important is the psychological effect on nonscientific minds, both white and yellow. People think things are wonderful that look wonderful. The average American is completely unimpressed by scientific wonders; he expects them, takes them as a matter of course with an attitude of 'So what? That's what you guys are paid for.'

"But add a certain amount of flubdub and hokum and *don't* label it 'scientific' and he will be impressed. It's wonderful advertising."

"Well," said Calhoun, dismissing the matter, "no doubt you know best—you have evidently had a great deal of experience in fooling the public. I've never turned my attention to such matters; my concern is with pure science. If you no longer need me here, Major, I have work to do."

"Certainly, Colonel, certainly! Go right ahead, your work is of prime importance . . .

"Still," he added meditatively, when Calhoun had gone, "I don't see why mass psychology shouldn't be a scientific field. If some of the scientists had taken the trouble to formulate some of the things that salesmen and politicans know already, we might never have gotten into the mess we're in."

"I think I can answer that," Dr. Brooks said diffidently.

"Huh? Oh, yes, Doctor—what were you going to say?"

"Psychology is not a science because it is too difficult. The scientific mind is usually orderly, with a natural love for order. It resents and tends to ignore fields in which order is not readily apparent. It gravitates to fields in which order is easily found such as the physical sciences, and leaves the more complex fields to those who play by ear, as it were. Thus we have a rigorous science of thermodynamics but are not likely to have a science of psychodynamics for many years yet to come."

Wilkie swung around so that he faced Brooks. "Do you really believe that, Brooksie?"

"Certainly, my dear Bob."

Ardmore rapped on his desk, "It's an interesting subject, and I wish we could continue the discussion— but it looks like rain, and the crops still to get in. Now about this matter of founding a church in Denver—anybody got any ideas?"

CHAPTER SIX

WILKIE SAID, "I'M GLAD I DON'T HAVE TO TACKLE IT. I wouldn't have the slightest idea where to start."

"Ah, but you may have to tackle it, Bob," Ardmore countered. "We may all have to tackle it. Damn it—if we only had a few hundred that we could depend on! But we haven't; there are only nine of us." He sat still for a moment, drumming the table. "Just nine."

"You'll never get Colonel Calhoun to make noises like a preacher," commented Brooks.

"Okay, then—eight. Jeff, how many cities and towns are there in the United States?"

"And you can't use Frank Mitsui," persisted Brooks. "For that matter, while I'm willing enough I don't see how you can use me. I haven't any more idea of how to go about setting up a fake church than I have about how to teach ballet dancing."

"Don't fret about it, Doctor, neither have I. We'll play by ear. Fortunately there aren't any rules. We can cook it up to suit ourselves."

"But how are you going to be convincing?"

"We don't have to be convincing—not in the sense of getting converts. Real converts might prove to be a nuisance. We just have to be convincing enough to look like a legitimate religion to our overlords. And that doesn't have to be very convincing. All religions look equally silly from the outside. Take the—" Ardmore caught a look on Scheer's face and said, "Sorry! I don't mean to tread on anybody's toes. But it's a fact just the same and one that we will make military use of. Take any religious mystery, any theological proposition: expressed in ordinary terms it will read like sheer nonsense to the outsider, from the ritualistic, symbolic eating of human flesh and blood practiced by all the Christian sects to the outright cannibalism practiced by some savages."

"Wait a minute, now!" he went on. "Don't throw anything at me. I'm not passing judgments on *any* religious beliefs or practices; I'm just pointing out that we are free to do anything at all, so long as we call it a religious practice and so long as we don't tread on the toes of the monkey men. But we have to decide what it is we are going to do and what it is we are going to say."

"It's not the double-talk that worries me," said Thomas. "I just stuck to saying nothing in big words and it worked out all right. It's the matter of getting an actual toe hold in the cities. We just haven't got enough people to do it. Was that what you were thinking about when you asked me how many cities and towns there are in the country?"

"Mmm, yes. We can't act—we don't *dare* act, until we cover the United States like a blanket. We'll have to make up our minds to a long war."

"Major, why do you want to cover every city and town?"

Ardmore looked interested. "Keep talking."

"Well," Thomas went on diffidently, "from what we've already learned the PanAsians don't maintain real military force in every hamlet. There are between sixty and seventy-five places that they have garrisoned. Most towns just have a sort of combination tax collector, mayor, and chief of police to see that the orders of the Hand are carried out. The local panjandrum isn't even a soldier, properly speaking, even though he goes armed and wears a uniform. He's sort of an M.P., a civil servant acting as a military governor. I think we can afford to ignore him; his power wouldn't last five minutes if he weren't backed up by the troops and weapons in the garrisoned cities."

Ardmore nodded. "I see your point. You feel that we should concentrate on the garrisoned towns and cities and ignore the rest. But look, Jeff—we mustn't underestimate the enemy. If the Great God Mota shows up nowhere but in the garrisoned spots it's going to look mighty funny to some intelligence officer among the PanAsians when he gets to fiddling with the statistics of the occupied country. I think we've *got* to show up elsewhere and anywhere."

"And I respectfully suggest that we can't, sir. We haven't men enough to pull it off. We'll have trouble enough recruiting and training enough men to set up a temple in each of the garrisoned cities."

Ardmore chewed a thumbnail and looked frustrated. "You're probably right. Well, confound it, we won't get anywhere at all if we sit here worrying about the difficulties. I said we'd have to play by ear and that's what we'll do. The first job is to get a headquarters set up in Denver. Jeff, what are you going to need?"

Thomas frowned. "I don't know. Money, I suppose."

"No trouble about that," said Wilkie. "How much? I can make you half a ton of gold as easily as half a pound."

"I don't think I can carry more than about fifty pounds."

"I don't think he can spend bullion very easily," Ardmore commented. "It should be in coin."

"I can use bullion," Thomas insisted. "All I have to do is to take it to the Imperial bank. Panning gold is encouraged; our gracious masters charge one hell of a stiff seigniorage."

Ardmore shook his head. "You're missing the propaganda aspect. A priest in long robes and a flowing beard doesn't whip out a check book and a fountain pen; it's out of character. I don't want you to have a bank account anyhow; it will give the enemy detailed records of just what you are doing. I want you to pay for things with beautiful, shiny golden coins, stacks of them. It will make a tremendous impression. Scheer, are you any good at counterfeiting?"

"I've never tried it, sir."

"No time like the present. Every man needs an

alternative profession. Jeff, you didn't have any chance to pick up an Imperial gold coin, did you? We need a model."

"No, I didn't. But I suppose I could get one, if I sent word out among the 'bos that I needed one."

"I hate to wait. But you've got to have money to tackle Denver."

"Does it have to be Imperial money?" asked Doctor Brooks.

"Eh?"

The biologist hauled a five dollar gold piece from his pocket. "Here's a lucky piece I've carried since I was a kid. I guess this is a lucky time to let it go."

"Hmm . . . How about it, Jeff? Can you pass American money?"

"Well, American paper money is no good, but gold coin— My guess is that those leeches probably won't object, so long as it's gold—at the bullion price, at least. I'm sure that Americans will take it."

"We don't care how much they discount it." Ardmore took the coin and chucked it to Scheer. "How long will it take you to make forty or fifty pounds of those?"

The master sergeant studied it. "Not long if I pour them rather than stamp them. You want them all just alike, sir?"

"Why not?"

"Well, sir, there's the matter of the date."

"Oh! I get you. Well, that's the only pattern we have; I guess we'll just have to hope that they either won't notice or won't care."

"If you can allow me just a little more time I think I could fix it, sir. I make about twenty or so with this as a pattern, then I'll do a little hand work and put a different date on each one. That will give me twenty different patterns instead of one."

"Scheer, you have the soul of an artist. Do it that way. While you are about it, you had better vary the scratches and wear marks on each."

"I had thought of that, sir."

Ardmore grinned. "This team is going to be a headache to His Imperial Nastiness yet. Well, how about it, Jeff? Any more points to settle before we adjourn the meeting?"

"Just one, boss. How do I get to Denver? Or how do we get there, assuming that Howe comes along?"

"I thought you would bring that up. It's a sticky question; we can't expect the Hand to provide you with a helicopter. How are your feet? Any broken arches? Corns and bunions?"

"I'll be switched if I want to walk. It's a long way."

"Don't blame you. And the devil of it is that it's a problem we're going to have with us from now on, if we are going to organize all over the country."

"I don't understand the difficulty," put in Brooks. "I thought citizens were still allowed to ride anything but aircraft?"

"Sure—with travel permits and endless red tape. Never mind," Ardmore continued, "the day will come when the costume of a priest of Mota will be all the travel permit we'll need. If we work this right, we'll be teacher's pet with all sorts of special privileges. In the meantime the trick is to get Jeff into Denver without attracting undue attention and without wearing out his feet. Say, Jeff, you never did tell me how you traveled. Somehow we missed that."

"I hitch-hiked. Quite a chore, too. Most of the truckers are too scared of the security police to risk it."

"You did? You shouldn't have, Jeff. The priests of Mota do not hitch-hike. It doesn't fit in with miracle working."

"Well, what do they do? Dawggone it, Major, if I had walked I would still be on the way—or more likely arrested by some flunky who hadn't gotten the news yet." Thomas' face showed irritation most unusual in him.

"Sorry. I shouldn't second-guess you. But we will have to figure out a better way."

"Why don't I just run him down in one of the scout cars?" asked Wilkie. "At night, of course."

"Night doesn't mean anything to radar, Bob. They would shoot you out of the sky."

"I don't think so. We have an almost unlimited amount of power at our disposal—sometimes it scares me when I try to think how much. I believe I can rig a radar beacon effect that will burn out any radar set that is turned on us."

"Giving notice to the enemy that there is still someone around capable of hanky-panky with electronics? We mustn't tip our hand so soon, Bob."

Wilkie shut up, crestfallen. Ardmore thought it over. "And yet we've got to take chances. You rig your rig, Bob—then plan on hedgehopping all the way. We'll do it about three or four o'clock in the morning and there's a chance that you won't be noticed at all. Use your rig if you have to but if you do then *everyone* is to return to base. The incident must not be connected with the priests of Mota, even in the matter of timing. The same applies after Wilkie sets you down, Jeff. If by any chance you are surprised, use the Ledbetter effect to kill off all the enemy anywhere close to you—then go underground. Jungle up. Under no circumstances is any PanAsian to be permitted to suspect that the priests of Mota are anything but what they seem. Kill off your witnesses and escape."

"Right, boss."

The little scout car hovered over Lookout Mountain a few feet away from Buffalo Bill's grave. The door opened and a robed priest dropped to the ground, stumbling because of the heavy money belt slung from his shoulders and waist. A similar figure followed him and landed a bit more surefootedly. "You all right, Jeff?"

"Sure."

Wilkie left the car on automatic long enough to lean out and say, "Good luck!"

"Thanks. But shut up and get going."

"Okay." The door closed and the car disappeared into the night.

It was growing light by the time Thomas and Howe reached the foot of the mountain and started into Denver. So far as they knew they had not been detected although once they had crouched in bushes for several minutes, afraid to breathe, while a patrol passed. Jeff had kept his staff ready, a thumb resting lightly on a golden leaf in the decorations below the cube of Mota. But the patrol passed on, unaware of the curbed lightnings trained on them.

Once in the city and in daylight they made no

further attempt to avoid attention. Few PanAsians were about so early; members of the slave race scurried along the streets, on their way to their labors, but the master race still slept. The Americans who saw them stared briefly but did not stop them nor speak to them; native Americans had already learned the first law of police states: mind your own business; don't be nosy!

Jeff deliberately sought out an encounter with a PanAsian policeman. He and Alec stepped down from the curb, switched on their shields and waited. No Americans were nearby; the presence of occupation police caused them to melt into walls. Jeff wet his lips and said "I'll do the talking, Alec."

"Suits me."

"Here he comes. Oh, my god, Alec, switch on your halo!"

"Huh?" Howe reached a finger up under his turban behind his right ear; the halo, shimmering iridescent light, sprang into being over his head. It was a mere ionization effect, a parlor trick of the additional spectra, less mysterious than natural aurora— but it looked good.

"That's better," Jeff acknowledged, from the side of his mouth. "What's the matter with your beard?"

"It keeps coming unstuck. I sweat."

"Don't let it come unstuck now! Here he comes—" Thomas struck the benediction pose; Howe followed suit. Jeff intoned, "Peace be unto you, Master!"

The Asiatic cop stopped. His knowledge of English was limited to *halt*, *come along*, and *show your card;* he depended on his club to keep the dogs in line. On the other hand he recognized the get up; it matched a picture on a notice newly posted in the barracks—this was one of the many silly things the slaves were allowed to do.

Still, a slave was a slave and must be kept in line. All slaves must bow; these slaves were not bowing. He cracked his club at the midriff of the nearer slave.

The nightstick bounced off before it reached the robed figure; the cop's fingers tingled as if he swung on something quite hard. "Peace be unto you!" Jeff rumbled again and watched him narrowly. The fellow was armed with a vortex pistol; Jeff was not afraid of it but it was no part of his plan to let the creature discover that he was immune to the Emperor's weapons. He was sorry that he had to use the shield against a blow from a stick and hoped that the PanAsian would not be able to believe the evidence of his own senses.

Certainly the man was startled. He looked at his stick, started to draw it back as if to swing again, then appeared to change his mind. He resorted to his meager supply of English. "Come along!"

Jeff raised his hand again. "Peace be unto you! It is not meet that the farjon should ripsnipe the cuskapads in the sight of the great lord Mota! Franchope!" He pointed to Howe.

The cop looked doubtful, then moved a few feet away to the street corner, glanced up and down and blew his whistle. Alec whispered, "What did you point to *me* for?"

"I don't know. It seemed like a good idea. Watch it!"

Another cop came trotting up; the pair approached

Howe and Thomas. The new one seemed to be in authority over the first; they held a short discussion in meaningless singsong, then the later arrival came close, drawing his pistol as he did so. "You fellow boys, come along now quick!"

"Come, Alec." Thomas fell in with the policemen, switching off his shield as he did so. He hoped that Alec would notice that he had done so and conformed, it seemed a good notion not to advertise the existence of the shields—not yet, at least.

The PanAsian conducted them to the nearest police station. Jeff walked briskly along, giving unctuous blessings to one and all. As they neared the station the senior cop sent the other trotting on ahead. When the party arrived they found the officer in charge waiting in the doorway, apparently curious to see these queer fish his men had hooked.

He was both curious and very much on his toes; the officer knew the circumstances under which the unfortunate lieutenant who had first turned up these strange holy men had gone to his ancestors. He was determined not to make a mistake which would cause him to lose face.

Jeff marched up to him, struck his pose and said, "Peace be unto you! Master, I have a complaint to make about your servants. They have stopped us from carrying out our holy work, work which is blessed by His Serene Highness himself, the Imperial Hand!"

The officer fingered his swagger stick, then spoke in his own language to his subordinates. He turned back to Jeff. "Who are you?"

"A priest of the great god Mota."

The PanAsian asked the same question of Alec; Jeff

interceded. "Master," he said hastily, "he is a most holy man who has taken a vow of silence. If you force him to break it the sin will be on your head."

The officer hesitated. The bulletin concerning these crazy savages had been most pointed, but it had given no clear precedents for dealing with them. He hated to establish precedents; those who did so were sometimes promoted, more frequently they joined their ancestors. "He need not break his holy vow. But show me your cards, both of you."

Jeff looked amazed. "We are humble, nameless holy men, serving the great god Mota. What have we to do with such?"

"Hurry up!"

Jeff tried to look sad rather than nervous. He had rehearsed this speech in his mind; much depended on it getting across. "I am sorry for you, young Master. I will pray to Mota on your behalf. But now I must insist that you take me before the Hand of the Emperor—at once!"

"That's impossible."

"His Highness has seen me before; he will see me again. The Hand of the Emperor is always ready to see the servers of the great god Mota."

The officer looked at him, turned and went back into the station house. They waited.

"Do you suppose he'll actually have us taken before the prince?" Howe whispered.

"I hope not. I don't think so."

"Well, what will you do if he does?"

"Whatever I have to. Shut up—you're supposed to be under a vow of silence."

The officer came back after several minutes and said curtly, "You are free to go."

"To the Imperial Hand?" Jeff inquired maliciously.

"No, no! Just go. Get out of my district."

Jeff stepped back one pace and delivered a last benediction. The two "priests" turned away. From the corner of his eye Jeff saw the officer lift his swagger stick and cut savagely at the senior of the two policemen; he pretended not to see. He walked about a block before he spoke to Howe. "There! We should have no more trouble for a while."

"How do you figure? You sure got him sore at us."

"That's not the point. We can't afford to have him or any other cop thinking he can push us around like the others. By the time we have gone three blocks the word will be all over town that I'm back and to lay off. That's the way we've got to have it."

"Maybe so. I still think it's dangerous to have the cops on the alert for us."

"You don't understand," Jeff said impatiently. "There isn't any other safe way to do it. Cops are cops, no matter what is the color of their skin. They deal in fear and they understand fear. Once they understand we can't be touched, that it is very bad medicine to bother us, they'll be as polite to us as they are to their superiors. You'll see."

"I hope you're right."

"I'm right. Cops are cops. Pretty soon we'll have them on our payroll. Oh, oh! Watch it, Alec—here comes another one." A PanAsian policeman was dog-trotting up behind them. However, instead of over-taking them or calling to them to halt, he crossed over and kept abreast with them on the other side of the street. He ignored them determinedly.

"What's up, d'you think, Jeff?"

"We're being chaperoned. A good thing, Alec— the rest of the monkeys won't bother us now. We'll just get on with our job. You know this town pretty well, don't you? Where do you think we ought to locate the temple?"

"I guess that depends on what you are looking for."

"I don't know exactly." He stopped and wiped sweat from his face; the robes were hot and the money belt made it worse. "Now that I'm here, this whole deal seems silly. I guess I wasn't meant to be a secret agent. How about out in the west end, in the expensive neighborhood? We want to make a big impression."

"No, I don't think so, Jeff. There are just two kinds of people out in the rich neighborhoods now."

"Yes?"

"PanAsians and traitors—black market dealers and other sorts of collaborationists."

Thomas looked shocked. "I guess I've been out of circulation too long. Alec, until this very minute it never occurred to me that an American—*any* American—would go along with the invaders."

"Well, I wouldn't have believed it either, if I hadn't seen it. I guess some people will do anything, born pimps."

They settled on an empty warehouse downtown near the river in a populous, poor neighborhood. The area had long been rundown; now it was depressed. Three out of four shops were boarded up;

trade had stagnated. The building was one of many empty warehouses; Thomas picked it because of its almost cubical shape, matching that of the mother temple and the cube on his staff, and the fact that it was detached from other buildings by an alley on one side and a vacant lot on the other.

The main door was broken. They peered in, entered and snooped around. The place was a mess but the plumbing was intact and the walls were sound. The ground floor was a single room with a twenty foot ceiling and few pillars; it would do for "worship."

"I think it will do," Jeff decided. A rat jumped out of a pile of rubbish heaped against one wall. Almost absentmindedly he trained his staff on it; the animal leaped high and dropped dead. "How do we go about buying it?"

"Americans can't own real estate. We'll have to find out what official holds the squeeze on it."

"That oughtn't to be hard." They went outside; their police chaperone waited across the street. He looked the other way.

The streets were fairly well filled by now, even in this neighborhood. Thomas reached out and snagged a passing boy—a child of not more than twelve but with the bitter, knowing eyes of a cynical man. "Peace be unto you, son. Who rents this building?"

"Hey, you let go of me!"

"I mean you no harm." He handed the boy one of Scheer's best five dollar gold pieces.

The boy looked at it, let his eyes slide past them to the Asiatic guard across the street. The PanAsian did not seem to be watching; the lad caused the coin to disappear. "Better see Konsky. He has all the angles on things like that."

"Who is Konsky?"

"Everybody knows Konsky. Say, granpa, what's the idea of the funny clothes? The slanties'll make trouble for you."

"I am a priest of the great god Mota. The Lord Mota takes care of his own. Take us to this Konsky."

"Nothing doing. I don't want to tangle with the slanties." The boy tried to wriggle away; Jeff held his arm firmly and produced another coin. He did not hand it over.

"Fear not. The Lord Mota will protect you, too."

The youngster looked at it, glanced around, and said, "Okay. Come along."

He led them around a corner and to a walk-up office building located over a saloon. "He's up there if he's in." Jeff gave the boy the second coin and told him to come see him again, at the warehouse, as the Lord Mota had gifts for him. Alec questioned the wisdom of this as they climbed the stairs.

"The kid's all right," said Jeff. "Sure, the things that have happened to him have turned him into a guttersnipe. But he's on our side. He'll advertise us—and not to the PanAsians."

Konsky turned out to be a blandly suspicious man. It was soon evident that he "had connections," but he was slow to talk until he saw the red gold color of money. After that he was not in the least put off by the odd dress and odd manners of his clients (Thomas gave him the full treatment, with benedictions thrown in, aware that Konsky would discount it but for the purpose of staying in character). He made sure of the building Thomas meant, dickered over the rental and the bribe—he called it "charges for special services"—and left them.

Thomas and Howe were glad to be left alone. Being a "holy man" had disadvantages; they had had nothing to eat since leaving the Citadel. Jeff dug sandwiches out from under his robes; they munched them. Best of all, there was a washroom adjoining Konsky's office.

Three hours later they were in possession of a document, the English translation of which stated that the Heavenly Emperor was graciously pleased to grant to his faithful subjects etc., etc.,—a lease paid up on the warehouse. In exchange for another unreasonable amount of money Konsky agreed to stir up enough labor to clean the place at once, that very day, and to provide certain repairs and materials. Jeff thanked him and with a straight face invited him to attend the first services to be held in the new temple.

They trudged back to the warehouse. Once out of Konsky's earshot Jeff said, "Y' know, Alec, we're going to make lots of use of that character—but when the day comes, well, I've got a little list and he's at the top of it. I mean to take care of him myself."

"Split him with me," was Howe's only comment.

The street urchin popped up from nowhere when they reached the warehouse. "Any more errands, granpa?"

"Bless you, son. Yes, several." After another financial transaction the boy left to find cots and bedding for them. Jeff watched his departure and said, "I think I'll make an altar boy out of that kid. He can go places and do things that we can't—and the cops aren't so likely to stop a person that age."

"I don't think you should trust him."

"I won't. So far as he will ever know we are a couple of crackpots, firmly convinced that we are priests of the great god Mota. We can't afford to trust anybody, Alec, until we are sure of them. Come on—let's kill all the rats in this place before the cleaners get here. Want me to check the setting on your staff?"

By nightfall the First Temple of Denver of the Lord Mota was a going concern, even though it still looked like a warehouse and had no congregation. The place reeked of disinfectant, the rubbish was gone, and the front door would lock. There were two beds of sorts and groceries enough to last two men a fortnight.

Their chaperone from the police force was still across the street.

The police guard stayed with them for four days. Twice squads of police came and searched through the place. Thomas let them; as yet there was nothing to hide. Their staffs were still their only source of power and the only Ledbetter communicator they had with them gave Howe a slightly hunch-backed appearance in the day time; he wore it while Thomas wore the money belt.

In the meantime through Konsky they acquired a fast and powerful ground car—and permission to drive it, or have it driven, anywhere in the jurisdiction of the Hand. The "charge for special services" was quite high. The driver they hired for it was *not* acquired through Konsky, but indirectly through Peewee Jenkins, the boy who had helped them on the first day.

The watch was withdrawn from them around noon on the fourth day. That afternoon Jeff left Howe to hold the place and went back to the Citadel by car. He returned with Scheer, who looked vastly uncomfortable and out of character in priestly vestments and beard but who bore with him a cubical chest enameled in the six sacred colors of Mota. Once inside the warehouse with the door locked Scheer opened the chest with great care and in a particular fashion which prevented it from exploding and taking them and the building with it. He got very busy on the newly constructed "altar." He finished shortly after midnight; there was more work to do outside, with Thomas and Howe standing guard, ready to stun or kill if necessary to prevent the sergeant being interupted.

The morning sun fell on a front wall of emerald green, the other walls were red and golden and deep sky blue. The temple of Mota was ready for converts— and for others.

Most important, none but a Caucasian could now pass through its door with impunity.

An hour before daylight Jeff posted himself at the door and waited nervously. The sudden transformation was sure to stir up another search squad; if necessary he must stop them, stun, or even kill—but no search could be permitted. He hoped to dissuade; the temple must be established as an enclave used only by the slave race. But a slight excess of zeal on the part of an underling could force him to violent means, and thereby destroy the hope of peaceful penetration.

Howe came up behind him and made him jump. "Uh? Oh—Alec! Don't do that. I'm nervous as a cat already."

"Sorry. Major Ardmore is on the circuit. He wants to know how you are making out."

"You'll have to talk to him. I can't leave the door."

"He wants to know when Scheer will be back, too."

"Tell him I'll send him back just as soon as I know it's safe to step outside this door and not a minute sooner."

"O.K." Howe turned away. Jeff looked back at the street and felt the hair on his neck stand up. A PanAsian in uniform was staring curiously at the building. The foreigner stood for a moment, then went away at the dog trot they all affected when moving on duty.

"Mota, old boy," Jeff said to himself. "It's time to do your stuff."

Less than ten minutes later a squad arrived commanded by the same officer who had searched the building before. "Stand aside, Holy One."

"No, Master," Jeff said firmly, "the temple is now consecrated. None may enter but worshipers of the Lord Mota."

"We will not harm your temple, Holy One. Stand aside."

"Master, if you enter I cannot save you from the wrath of the Lord Mota. Nor can I save you from the wrath of the Imperial Hand." Before the officer had time to turn this over in his mind Jeff went quickly on, "The Lord Mota expected this visit from you and greets you. He bids me, his humble servant, to make you three gifts."

"Gifts?"

"For yourself—" Jeff laid a heavy purse in his hand. "For your superior officer, may his name be blessed—" A second purse followed. "—and for your men." A third purse was added; the PanAsian was forced to use both hands.

He stood there for a moment. There could be no doubt in his mind, from the weight alone, as to what the purses contained. It was more gold than he had ever handled in his life. Shortly he turned, barked an order at his men, and strode away.

Howe came up again. "You made it, Jeff?"

"This round, at least." Thomas watched the squad move up the street. "Cops are all alike, the world over. Reminds me of a railroad dick I once knew."

"Do you think he'll share it out the way you suggested?"

"The men won't get any, that's sure. He may split with his boss, to keep him quiet. He'll probably find some way to hide the third lot of loot before he gets back to the station. What I'm wondering is: is he an *honest* politician?"

"Huh?"

" 'An honest politician is one that stays bought.' Come on, let's get ready for customers."

They held their first services that evening. As church services they were nothing much, since Jeff was still feeling out the art. They conformed to the good old skid-road mission principle: sing a hymn and eat a meal. But the meal was good red meat and white bread—and the recipients had not eaten that well in many months.

CHAPTER SEVEN

"HELLO? HELLO? JEFF, ARE YOU THERE? CAN YOU hear me?"

"Sure I can hear you. Don't shout, Major."

"I wish these damn rigs were regular telephones. I like to *see* a man I'm talking to."

"If they were ordinary phones our Asiatic pals could listen in on us. Why don't you ask Bob and the colonel to whip up a vision circuit? I'll bet they could do it."

"Bob has already done so, Jeff, but Scheer is so busy machining parts for altar installations that I don't like to ask him to make it. Do you suppose you could recruit some assistants for Scheer? A machinist or two, maybe, and a radio technician? The manufacturing end of this enterprise is geting out of hand and Scheer is going to crack up from overwork.

Every night I have to go around and order him to go to bed."

Thomas thought about it. "I have one man in mind. Used to be a watchmaker."

"A watchmaker! That's swell!"

"I don't know. He's a little bit balmy; his whole family was wiped out. A sad case, almost as sad as Frank Mitsui. Say, how is Frank? Is he feeling any better?"

"Seems to be. Not down inside of course, but he seems happy enough at his work. He's taken over the kitchen and the clerical work you used to do for me, both."

"Give him my best."

"I will. Now about this watchmaker—you don't have to be as careful in recruiting personnel for the Citadel as you have to be in picking field workers, since once they are inside they can't get out."

"I know that, boss. I didn't use any special tests when I sent you Estelle Devens. Of course I wouldn't have sent her if she hadn't been about to be shipped out as a pleasure girl."

"You did all right. Estelle is a fine woman. She helps Frank in the kitchen, she helps Graham sew the robes, and Bob Wilkie is training her as a pararadio operator." Ardmore chuckled. "Sex is rearing its interesting head. I think Bob is sweet on her."

Thomas's voice was suddenly grave. "How about that, boss? Is it likely to louse things up?"

"I don't think so. Bob is a gentleman and Estelle is a nice girl if I ever saw one. If biology starts getting in the way of their work, I'll just up and marry them, in my capacity as high priest of the supercolossal god Mota."

"Bob won't go for that. He's a bit of a puritan, if you ask me."

"All right then, in my capacity as chief magistrate of this thriving little village. Don't be stuffy. Or send me up a real preacher."

"How about sending up more women, Major? I sent Estelle on impulse, more or less, but there are many more young women just as badly in need of help as she was."

There was a long wait before Ardmore replied, "Captain, that is a very difficult question. Most reluctantly I am forced to say that this is a military organization at war, not a personal rescue mission. Unless a female is being recruited for a military function to which she is adapted, you are not to recruit her, even to save her from the PanAsians' pleasure cities."

"Yes, sir. I will comply. I shouldn't have sent Estelle."

"What's done is done. She's working out all right. Don't hesitate to recruit suitable women. This is going to be a long war and I think we can maintain morale better with a mixed organization than with a strictly stag setup. Men without women go to pieces; they lose purpose. But try to make the next one an older woman, something between a mother superior and a chaperone. An elderly trained nurse would be the type. She could be lab assistant to Brooks and house mother to the babes, both."

"I'll see what I can find."

"And send up that watchmaker. We really need him."

"I'll give him a hypo test tonight."

"Is that necessary, Jeff? If the PanAsians killed his family you can be sure of his sentiments."

"That's *his* story. I'll feel a lot safer if I hear him tell it when he's doped. He might be a ringer you know."

"O.K., you're right, as usual. You run your show; I'll run mine. When are you going to be able to turn the temple over to Alec, Jeff? I need you here."

"Alec could take it now, just to run it. But as I understand it, my prime duty is to locate and recruit more 'priests,' ones capable of going out in the field and starting a new cell alone."

"That's true, but can't Alec do that? After all, the final tests will be given here. We agreed that never, under any circumstances, would the true nature of what we are doing be revealed to anyone except after we got him inside the Citadel and under our thumbs. If Alec makes a mistake in picking a man it won't be fatal."

Jeff turned over in his mind what he wanted to say. "Look, boss, it may seem simple from where you sit; it doesn't look simple from here. I—" He paused.

"What's the matter, Jeff? Got the jitters?"

"I guess so."

"Why? It seems to me the operation is proceeding according to plan."

"Well, yes—maybe. Major, you said this would be a long war."

"Yes?"

"Well, it *can't* be. If it's a long war, we'll lose it."

"But it's *got* to be. We don't dare move until we have enough trusted people to strike all over the country at once."

"Yes, yes, but that's got to be the shortest possible time. What would you say was the greatest danger that faces us?"

"Huh? Why the chance that someone might give us away, either accidentally or on purpose."

"I don't agree, sir—not at all. That's your opinion because you see it from the Citadel. From here I see an entirely different danger—and it worries me all the time."

"Well, what is it, Jeff? Give."

"The worst danger—and it hangs like a sword over our heads all the time—is that the PanAsian authorities may grow suspicious of us. They may decide that we can't be what we pretend to be—just another phony western religion, good to keep the slaves quiet. If they once get that idea before we are ready, we're finished."

"Don't let it get you nervy, Jeff. In a pinch, you've got enough stuff to fight your way back to base. They can't use an atom bomb on you in one of their own capitals—and Calhoun says that the new shield on the Citadel will stop even an atom bomb."

"I doubt it. But what good would it do us if it did? Suppose we could hole up there until we died of old age: if we don't dare stick our noses out we can't win back the country!"

"Mmm . . . no—but it might give us time to think of something else."

"Don't kid yourself, Major. If they catch on, we're

licked—and the American people lose their last chance this generation, at least. There are still too few of us, no matter what weapons Calhoun and Wilkie can cook up."

"Suppose I concede your point: you knew all this when you went out. Why the panic? Battle fatigue?"

"You can call it that. But I want to discuss the dangers as I see them here in the field. If we really were a religious sect, with no military power, they'd leave us alone till hell froze. Right?"

"Check."

"Then the danger lies in the things we have to do to cover up the fact that we've got a lot of stuff we aren't supposed to have. Those dangers are all out here in the field. First—" Thomas ticked them off on his fingers, oblivious to the fact that his commanding officer could not see him. "—is the shield of the temple. We've *got* to have it; this place can't stand a search. But it would be almost as bad if we had to use it. If any senior PanAsian gets the notion to inspect in spite of our immunity, school is out for sure; I don't dare kill him and I don't dare let him come in. So far, by the grace of God, a lot of double-talk, and the liberal use of bribes, I've been able to turn them away."

"They already know that we've got the temple shields, Jeff; they've known it from the first day we made contact here."

"Do they, now? I don't think so. Thinking back over my interview with the Hand I'm convinced that that officer who tried to force his way into the mother temple wasn't believed when he made his report. And you can bet your last cookie he is dead now;

that's the way they work. The common soldiers that were there don't count. The second hazard is the personal shield that we 'priests' carry. I've used mine just once and I'm sorry I did. Fortunately he was just a common soldier, too. He wouldn't report it; he wouldn't be believed and he would lose face."

"But, Jeff, the 'priests' have got to wear shields; we can't let a staff fall into enemy hands—not to mention the fact that the monkeys might be able to drug an unshielded 'priest' before he could suicide."

"You're telling me! We've got to have them; we don't dare use them—and that calls for some fast double-talk in a pinch. The next hazard is the halo; the halo was a mistake, boss."

"Why do you say that?"

"O.K., it impresses the superstitious. But the bigshot PanAsians are no more superstitious than you are. Take the Hand—I wore it in his presence. He wasn't impressed; it was my great good luck that he apparently regarded it as nothing important, just a gadget to impress my followers. But suppose he had really thought about it and decided to find out how I did it?"

"Maybe," said Ardmore, "we had better omit the halo effect in the next city we penetrate."

"Too late. Our official designation here is 'holy men who wear halos.' It's our trademark."

"So? Jeff, I think you've done a wonderfully good job of covering up."

"There is one more hazard. It's a slow one, a time bomb."

"Eh?"

"Money. We've got too much money. That's a suspicious circumstance."

"But you had to have money to operate."

"How well I know it. It has been the only thing that enabled us to get away with it so far. These people are even more corruptible than Americans, Chief; with us it is a frowned-upon dereliction; with them it's an essential part of their culture. A good thing, too—we now have the respected position of the goose that lays the golden eggs."

"But why do you call it a time bomb? Why is it a hazard at all?"

"Remember what happened to the goose in the story? Some day some smart laddie is going to wonder where the goose gets all that gold and take him apart to find out. In the meantime all the recipients of our cumshaw are closing their eyes to the suspicious circumstances and getting as much as they can while the getting is good. I'm betting that each one will keep his mouth shut about his take, as long as he can get away with it. I doubt if the Hand knows that we seem to have an unlimited supply of American gold coins. But some day he will find out; that's the time bomb element. Unless he can be bribed, too—in a polite way, of course—he will start some very embarrassing investigations. Somewhere up the line we'll run into an official more interested in knowing the facts than in sticking out his palm. Before that day rolls around we had better be set to move!"

"Hmm . . . I suppose so. Well, Jeff, do the best you can and get us some 'priest' recruits up here as fast as you can. If we had one hundred dependable men, as talented in handling people as you are, we could set 'D' Day a month from now. But it may take years and, as you say, events may trip us up before we can move."

"You can see why I have trouble finding 'priest' recruits? Loyalty isn't enough; a special aptitude for kidding the public is necessary. I learned it as a hobo. Alec really hasn't got it; he's too honest. However I may have one recruit now—a chap named Johnson."

"Yes? What about him?"

"He used to be a real estate salesman and he has a very convincing manner. The PanAsians put him out of business, of course, and he's anxious to avoid the labor camps. I've been feeling him out."

"Well, if you think he'll do, send him up. Perhaps I can look him over there."

"Huh?"

"I've been thinking while I listened. Jeff, I *don't* know enough about the field situation; I've got to come see for myself. If I am going to direct this show, I've got to understand it. I can't do it from a hole in the ground; I'm falling out of touch."

"I thought that was settled a long time ago, boss."

"What do you mean?"

"Are you going to leave Calhoun as acting C.O.?"

Ardmore remained silent for several moments, then said, "Damn you, Jeff!"

"Well, are you?"

"Oh, very well! Let's drop the matter!"

"Don't get sore, boss. I've been trying to give you the whole picture; that's why I've talked so long."

"I'm glad you did. I want you to repeat it, in much more detail. I'll put Estelle on and have her make a recording of everything you've got to say. We'll work up an instruction manual for student 'priests' from your lecture."

"O.K., but let me call you back. I've got a service in ten minutes."

"Can't Alec even run a service?"

"He does and he's O.K. He preaches a better sermon than I do. But it's my best recruiting time, Major; I study the crowd and talk to them individually afterwards."

"O.K., O.K.—I'm switching off."

" 'Bye."

Services were crowded by now. Thomas did not fool himself that the creed of the great god Mota was the drawing card; even while the service proceeded, at the sides of the hall tables were being piled high with food, purchased with Scheer's fine gold. But Alec put on a good show. It seemed to Jeff, as he listened to him preach, that the old mountain man had somehow reconciled his strange new job with his conscience so thoroughly that he actually believed that he was preaching his own religion, in symbols of course and with odd ritual—but his voice carried conviction.

"If he keeps that up," Jeff told himself, "we'll have women fainting in the aisles. Maybe I should tell him to soft-pedal it."

But without untoward incident Alec reached the final hymn. The congregation sang with verve, then trooped toward the tables. Sacred music had at first been a problem until Jeff had hit on the dodge of putting new words to the commonest American patriotic music. It served a double purpose; anyone who listened closely could hear the old words, the true words, being sung by the bolder spirits present.

Jeff circulated around among his flock while they ate, patting the heads of children, pronouncing blessings—and listening. As he passed a man got up from his place and stopped him. It was Johnson, the former real estate salesman. "A word with you, Holy One?"

"What is it, my son?"

Johnson indicated that he wanted to speak privately; they drew away from the crowd over into the shadow of the altar. "Holy One, I don't dare go back to my room tonight."

"Why not, my son?"

"I still haven't been able to get my work card validated. Today was my last day of grace. If I go home it's the camps for me."

Jeff looked grave. "You know that the servers of Mota do not preach resistance to mundane authority."

"You wouldn't turn me out to be arrested!"

"We do not refuse sanctuary. Perhaps it is not as bad as you think it is, my son; perhaps if you stay here tonight, tomorrow you may find someone to hire you and validate your card."

"I can stay, then?"

"You may stay." Thomas decided that Johnson might as well stay from then on; if he measured up, he would be sent to the Citadel for final test. If not, Johnson could stay as an unenlightened helper around the temple—the temple needed more help every day, especially in the kitchen.

When the crowd had gone Jeff locked the door,

then checked through the building personally to make sure that none but the resident help and those who had been granted overnight sanctuary were still inside. There were more than a dozen of these refugees; Jeff was studying some of them as prospective recruits.

Inspection completed and the place tidied up, Jeff shooed everyone but Alec upstairs to the second-floor dormitory rooms; he locked the door to the staircase after them. This was a nightly routine; the altar with its many marvelous gadgets was safe from snoopers, as it had a shield of its own, controlled by a switch in the basement—nonetheless Jeff did not want anyone attempting to get at it. The avowed reason for the nightly lock up was, of course, a piece of holy mumbo-jumbo having to do with the "sacredness" of the lower floor.

Alec and Jeff went down into the basement, locking after them a heavy, steel-sheathed door. Their apartment was a large room, housing the power unit for the altar, the communicator back to the base, and the same two cots Peewee Jenkins had gotten for them on their first day in Denver. Alec undressed, went into the adjoining bath, and got ready for bed. Jeff peeled off his robes and turban, but not his beard; it was now homegrown. He put on overalls, stuck a cigar in his mouth, and called the base.

For the next three hours he dictated, over Alec's snores. Then he, too, went to bed.

Jeff woke up with a feeling of unease. The lights had not switched on; therefore it was not the morning alarm that had wakened him. He lay very still for a moment, then reached down beside him on the floor and recovered his staff.

Someone was in the room, other than Alec, still snoring on the other cot. He knew it, although at the moment he could hear no sound. Working by touch alone he carefully set his shield to cover both cots. He switched on the lights.

Johnson was standing in front of the communicator. Some sort of complicated goggles covered his eyes; in his hand was a black-light projector.

"Stand where you are," Jeff said quietly.

The man whirled around, then shoved the goggles up on his forehead. He stood for a moment, blinking at the light.

Quite suddenly a vortex pistol appeared in his other hand. "Don't make any sudden moves, Pop," he snapped. "This is no toy."

"Alec!" Jeff called out. "Alec! Wake up."

Alec sat up, at once alert. He glanced around and dived for his staff. "I've got us both screened," Jeff said rapidly. "Now you grab him but don't kill him."

"Make a move and you get it," warned Johnson.

"Don't be foolish, my son," Jeff answered. "The great god Mota protects his own. Put down that gun."

Without wasting time on speech Alec was setting the controls on his staff. It took him some time; he had had only practice drills in the use of the tractor and pressor beams. Johnson watched him fumbling, looked uncertain, then fired at him point blank.

Nothing happened; Jeff's shield soaked up the energy.

Johnson looked amazed; he looked still more amazed

and rubbed his hand a moment later when Alec snatched the gun from his hand with a tractor beam. "Now," said Jeff, "tell us, my son, why you saw fit to violate the mysteries of Mota?"

Johnson looked around at him, his eyes showing apprehension but still defiant. "Stow that Mota stuff. I wasn't kidded."

"The Lord Mota is not mocked."

"Stow it, I tell you. How do you explain that stuff?" He hooked a thumb at the communicator.

"The Lord Mota need not explain. Sit down, my son, and make your peace with him."

"Sit down, my eye. I'm walking straight out of here. If you birds don't want this place swarming with slanties, you won't try to stop me. I wouldn't turn in a white man *unless* he made trouble for me."

"You are implying that you are a common thief?"

"Watch what you call me. You guys have been throwing gold around; anybody is bound to take an interest in it."

"Sit down."

"I'm leaving."

He turned away. Jeff said, "Nail him, Alec!—but don't hurt him."

The injunction slowed Alec down. Johnson was halfway up the stairs before Alec snatched his feet from under him. Johnson fell heavily, striking his head.

Unhurriedly Jeff got up and put on his robes. "Sit on him, Alec, with your staff. I'll reconnoiter." He went upstairs, was gone a few minutes, and returned. Johnson was stretched on Alec's cot, dormant. "Not much damage," Jeff reported. "The upper door's lock was merely picked. No one was awake; I relocked it. The lower door's lock will have to be replaced; he used something or other that melted it. That door really should have a shield; I must speak to Bob about that." He glanced at the figure. "Still out?"

"Not really. He was coming to; I gave him sodium pentothal."

"Good! I want to question him."

"So I figured."

"Anesthesia?"

"No, just a babble dose."

Thomas nipped one of Johnson's earlobes with a thumbnail and twisted viciously. The victim stirred. "Darn near anesthesia—must be the knock on his head. Johnson! Can you hear me?"

"Mmm, yes."

Thomas questioned him patiently for many minutes. Finally Alec stopped him. "Jeff, do we have to listen to any more of this? It's like staring down into a cesspool."

"It makes me want to vomit, too, but we've got to get the dope." He went on. Who paid him? What did the PanAsians expect to find out? How did he report back? When was he due to report next? Who else was in the organization? What did the PanAsians think of the temple of Mota? Did his boss know that he was here tonight?

And finally: what had induced him to go against his own people?

The drug was wearing off now. Johnson was almost aware of his surroundings, but his censors were still down and he spoke with a savage disregard of what his hearers might think of him. "A man's got to look out for himself, doesn't he? If you're smart you can get along anywhere."

"I guess we just aren't smart, Alec," Thomas commented. He sat still for several minutes, then said, "I think he's told us everything he knows. I'm trying to decide just what to do with him."

"If I give him another shot he may talk some more."

Johnson said, "You can't make me talk!" He seemed unaware that he already had talked.

Thomas struck him across the face with the back of his hand. "Shut up, you. You'll talk whenever we give you the needle. Right now you'll keep quiet." He went on to Alec, "There is a bare chance that they might get more out of him if we shipped him back to base. But I don't think so and it would be difficult and dangerous. If we got caught with him or if he escaped, the jig would be up. I think we had best dispose of him here and now."

Johnson looked stunned and tried to sit up, but Alec's staff kept him pinned to the cot. "Hey! What are you talking about? That's murder!"

"Give him another shot, Alec. We can't have him raising Cain while we work."

Howe said nothing, but quickly made the injection. Johnson tried to squirm away from it, then struggled a little before he gave in to the drug. Howe straightened up. His face was almost as disturbed as Johnson's had been. "Did you mean that the way it sounded, Jeff? If so, I didn't sign up for murder, either."

"It's not murder, Alec. We are executing a spy."

Howe chewed his lip. "It wouldn't bother me a

bit, I guess, to kill a man in a fair fight. But to tie him down and butcher him, like he was a hog, turns my stomach."

"Executions are always like that, Alec. Ever see a man die in a gas chamber?"

"But it *is* murder, Jeff. We don't have the authority to execute him."

"*I* have the authority, Alec. I am a commanding officer, acting independently, in war time."

"But consarn it, Jeff, you didn't even give him a drumhead court-martial."

"A trial is for the purpose of establishing guilt or innocence. Is he guilty?"

"Oh, he's guilty all right. But a man's entitled to a trial."

Jeff took a long breath. "Alec, I used to be a lawyer. The whole purpose of the complicated structure of western jurisprudence in criminal matters, as built up over the centuries, has been to keep the innocent from being convicted and punished through error. It sometimes lets the guilty go free in the process, but that's not the purpose. I don't have the personnel nor the time to form a military court and give this man a formal trial—but his guilt has been established with much more certainty than a court could possibly establish it and I don't propose to endanger my command and risk the ultimate outcome of the war by extending to him the protections that were devised to protect the innocent.

"If I could cut out his memory and turn him loose to report back that all he found was a screwy church and a lot of hungry people eating, I would do it, not to avoid the chore of killing him, but because it would confuse the enemy. I can't possibly turn him loose—"

"I didn't want you to do that, Jeff!"

"Shut up, soldier, and listen. If I turn him loose with the knowledge he has gained, the PanAsians will get it, the same way we made him talk, even if he tried to hold it back. We haven't the facilities to keep him here; it is dangerous to ship him back to base. I intend to execute him now." He paused.

Alec said diffidently, "Captain Thomas?"

"Yes?"

"Why don't you call up Major Ardmore and see what he thinks?"

"Because there is no reason to. If I have to ask him to make up my mind for me I'm no good on this job. I've just one thing more to add: you are too soft and mush-headed for this job. You apparently think that the United States can win this war without anyone getting hurt—you don't even have the guts to watch a traitor die. I had hoped to turn this command over to you shortly; instead I am shipping you back to the Citadel tomorrow with a report to the commander-in-chief that you are utterly unfit to be trusted with work in the face of the enemy. In the meantime you will carry out orders. Help me lug that hulk into the bathroom."

Howe's mouth quivered, but he said nothing. The two carried the unconscious man into the adjoining room. Before the temple was "consecrated" Thomas had had a partition knocked out between the janitor's toilet and the space adjoining and in that space had had an old-fashioned bath tub installed. They dumped him in the tub.

Howe wet his lips. "Why in the tub?"

"Because it will be a bloody mess."

"You aren't going to use your staff?"

"No, it would take me an hour to disassemble it and take out the suppressor circuit for the white-man band of frequencies. And I'm not sure I could get it back together right. Give me that straight razor of yours and get out."

Howe got the razor and came back. He did not hand it over. "You ever butchered a hog?" he inquired.

"No."

"Then I know more about how to do it." Stooping, he lifted Johnson's chin. The man breathed heavily and grunted. Howe made one quick slash and the man's throat was cut. He dropped the head, stood up and stared at the spreading red stream. He spat in it, then stepped to the wash stand and cleaned his razor.

Jeff said, "I guess I spoke too hastily, Alec."

Alec did not look up. "No," he said slowly, "not a bit too hastily. I guess it takes some time to get used to the notion of war."

"Yeah, I guess so. Well, let's dispose of this thing."

Despite a very short night Jeff Thomas was up unusually early as he wanted to report to Ardmore before the morning service. Ardmore listened carefully to the account, then said, "I'll send Scheer down to install a shield on the basement door. Some such rig will be standard for all temple installations from now on. How about Howe? Do you want to send him back?"

"No," Thomas decided, "I think he's over the hump now. He's squeamish by nature, but he's got plenty of moral courage. Damn it, boss, we've got to trust somebody."

"Are you willing to turn the temple over to him?"

"Well . . . yes, I am—now. Why?"

"Because I want you to move on to Salt Lake City practically at once. I lay awake most of the night thinking over what you told me yesterday. You stirred me up, Jeff; I had been getting fat and sloppy in my thinking. How many potential recruits have you got now?"

"Thirteen, now that Johnson is out of it. Not all of them candidates for 'priesthood,' of course."

"I want you to send them all here, at once."

"But, boss, I haven't examined them."

"I'm making a radical revision in procedure. We'll cut out examination under drugs except at the Citadel. You haven't the facilities to do it gracefully. I'm assigning Brooks to it; he will do all of it from now on and I will pass on the ones who get by his elimination. From now on the 'priests' will have the prime duty of locating likely candidates and sending them in to the mother temple."

Thomas thought about it. "How about characters like Johnson? We sure don't want his type penetrating into the Citadel."

"I've anticipated that—and that's why the examinations will be held here. A candidate will be doped before he goes to bed, but he won't know it. He will be given a hypo, roused, and examined during the night. If he passes, well and good. If he doesn't then he never will know he has been examined under drugs but he will be allowed to think that he has passed."

"Huh?"

"That's the beauty of it. He will be accepted into the service of the great god Mota, sworn in as a lay brother—and then we will work the tail off him! He'll sleep in a bare cell, scrub floors, eat poor food and damn little of it, and spend hours each day on his knees at his devotions. He'll be regimented so thoroughly that he will never have a chance to suspect that there is anything under this mountain but country rock. When he's got his bellyful, he will be sorrowfully allowed to give up his vows, then he can trot back and tell his Masters anything he jolly well pleases."

Thomas looked pleased. "It sounds swell, Major. It sounds like fun—and it sounds as if it would work."

"I think it will and it will turn their agents to our advantage. After the war is over we'll round them up and shoot 'em—the actual spies, I mean, not the soft heads. But that's a sideshow; let's talk about the candidates that pass. I want recruits and I want them fast. I want several hundred right away. Out of that several hundred I want to get at least sixty satisfactory candidates for 'priesthood'; I want to train them simultaneously and send them all out into the field at once. You've thoroughly sold me on the dangers of waiting, Jeff; I want to penetrate every major PanAsian center at the same time. You've convinced me that this is our only chance to pull off this masquerade."

Thomas whistled. "You don't want much, do you, boss?"

"It can be done. Here is the new doctrine for recruiting. Turn on your recorder."

"It's on."

"Good. Send in only such candidates as have lost immediate members of their families as a result of the PanAsian invasion, or have other superficial, *prima facie* evidences that they are likely to be loyal under stress. Eliminate obviously unstable persons but leave any other psychological elimination to the staff at the Citadel. Send in candidates from the following categories only: for the 'priesthood'—salesmen, advertising men, publicity men, newspapermen, preachers, politicians, psychologists, carnival pitch men or talkers, personnel managers, psychiatrists, trial lawyers, theatrical managers; for work not in contact with the public nor the enemy—skilled metal workers of all sorts, electronics technicians, jewelers, watchmakers, skilled precision workers in any engineering art, cooks, stenographers, laboratory technicians, physicists, seamstresses. Any of the latter group may be female."

"No female priests?"

"What do you think?"

"I'm against it. These babies rate women as zero or even minus. I don't think a female 'priest' could possibly operate in contact with them."

"I feel the same way. Now, can Alec take over the recruiting under this doctrine?"

"Hmm . . . boss, I hate to throw him on his own just yet."

"He wouldn't make a slip and give us away, would he?"

"No, but he might not get much in the way of results, either."

"Well, you'll just have to push him in, sink or swim. From here on we force the moves, Jeff. Turn the temple over to Alec and report here. You and Scheer will leave for Salt Lake City at once, publicly. Buy another car and use the driver you have now. Alec can recruit another driver. I want Scheer back here in forty-eight hours and I want your first recruits headed this way a couple of days thereafter. Two weeks from now I'll send someone out to relieve you, either Graham or Brooks—"

"Huh? Neither one of them has the temperament for it."

"They can pinch hit after you've broken the ground. We'll relieve the one I send as soon as possible with the proper type. You'll come back here and start a school for 'priests'—or, rather, continue it and improve it. I'm starting it now, with the people at hand. That's your job; I don't expect to send you into the field again, except possibly as a trouble shooter."

Thomas sighed. "I sure talked myself into a job, didn't I?"

"You did indeed. Get moving."

"Just a minute. Why Salt Lake City?"

"Because I think it's a good spot for recruiting. Those Mormons are shrewd, practical people and I don't think you'll find a traitor among them. If you work at it, I think you can convince their Elders that the great god Mota is a good thing to have around and no menace to their own faith. We haven't made half enough use of the legitimate churches; they should be the backbone of the movement. Take the Mormons—they run to lay missionaries; if you work it right you can recruit a number of them with such experience, courageous, used to organizing in hostile territory, good talkers, smart. Get it?"

Robert A. Heinlein

"I get you. Well, I'll sure try."

"You can do it. As soon as possible we'll send someone to relieve Alec and let him try his hand alone in Cheyenne. It's not a big place; if he flops it won't matter too much. But I'm betting he can take Cheyenne. Now you go take Salt Lake City."

CHAPTER EIGHT

DENVER, CHEYENNE, SALT LAKE CITY, PORTLAND,
Seattle, San Francisco. Kansas City, Chicago, Little
Rock. New Orleans, Detroit, Jersey City. Riverside,
Five Points, Butler, Hackettstown, Natick, Long
Beach, Yuma, Fresno, Amarillo, Grants, Parktown,
Bremerton, Coronado, Worcester, Wickenberg, Santa
Ana, Vicksburg, LaSalle, Morganfield, Blaisville,
Barstow, Wallkyll, Boise, Yakima, St. Augustine, Walla
Walla, Abilene, Chattahoochee, Leeds, Laramie,
Globe, South Norwalk, Corpus Christi.

"Peace be unto you! Peace, it's wonderful! Come,
all you sick and heavy laden! Come! Bring your
troubles to the temple of the Lord Mota. Enter the
sanctuary where the Masters dare not follow. Hold
up your heads as white men, for 'The Disciple is
Coming!'

"Your baby daughter is dying from typhoid? Bring

her in! Bring her in! Let the golden rays of Tamar make her well again. Your job is gone and you face the labor camps? Come in! Come in! Sleep on the benches and eat at the table that is never bare. There will be work aplenty for you to do; you can be a pilgrim and carry the word to others. You need only profit by instruction.

"Who pays for it all? Why, Lord love you, man, gold is the gift of Mota! Hurry! 'The Disciple is coming!' "

They poured in. At first they came through curiosity, because this new and startling and cockeyed religion was a welcome diversion from painful and monotonous facts of their slavelike existences. Ardmore's instinctive belief in flamboyant advertising justified itself in results; a more conventional, a more dignified cult would never have received the "house" that this one did.

Having come to be entertained, they came back for other reasons. Free food, and no questions asked—who minded singing a few innocuous hymns when they could stay for supper? Why, those priests could afford to buy luxuries that Americans rarely saw on their own tables, butter, oranges, good lean meat, paying for them at the Imperial storehouses with hard gold coin that brought smiles to the faces of the Asiatic bursars.

Besides that, the local priest was always good for a touch if a man was really hard up for the necessary. Why be fussy about creeds? Here was a church that did not ask a man to subscribe to its creeds; you could come and enjoy all the benefits and never be asked to give up your old-time religion—or even be asked if you had a religion. Sure, the priests and their acolytes appeared to take their god-with-six-attributes pretty seriously, but what of it? That was their business. Haven't we always believed in religious freedom? Besides, you had to admit they did good work.

Take Tamar, Lady of Mercy, now—maybe there was something to it. If you've seen a child choking to death with diphtheria, and seen it put to sleep by the server of Shaam, then washed in the golden rays of Tamar, and then seen it walk out an hour later, perfectly sound and whole, you begin to wonder. With half the doctors dead, with the army and a lot of the rest sent to concentration camps, anyone who could cure disease had to be taken seriously. What if it did look like superstitious mumbo-jumbo? Aren't we a practical people? It's results that count.

But cutting more deeply than the material advantages, were the psychological benefits. The temple of Mota was a place where a man could hold up his head and not be afraid, something he could not do even in his own home. "Haven't you heard? Why, they say that no flatface has ever set foot in one of their temples, even to inspect. They can't even get in by disguising themselves as white men; something knocks them out cold, right at the door. Personally, I think those apes are scared to death of Mota. I don't know what it is they've got, but you can breathe easy in the temple. Come along with me—you'll see!"

The Rev. Dr. David Wood called on his friend the equally reverend Father Doyle. The older man let him in himself. "Come in, David, come in," he

163

greeted him. "You're a pleasant sight. It's been too many days since I've seen you." He brought him into his little study and sat him down and offered tobacco. Wood refused it in a preoccupied manner.

Their conversation drifted in a desultory way from one unimportant subject to another. Doyle could see that Wood had something on his mind, but the old priest was accustomed to being patient. When it became evident that the younger man could not, or would not, open the subject, he steered him to it. "You seem like a man with something preying on his mind, David. Should I ask what it is?"

David Wood took the plunge. "Father, what do you think of this outfit that call themselves the priests of Mota?"

"Think of it? What should I think of it?"

"Don't evade me, Francis. Doesn't it matter to you when a heathen heresy sets up in business right under your nose?"

"Well, now, it seems to me that you have raised some points for discussion there, David. Just what is a heathen religion?"

Wood snorted. "You know what I mean! False gods! Robes, and bizarre temple, and—mummeries!"

Doyle smiled gently. "You were about to say 'papist mummeries,' were you not, David? No, I can't say that I am greatly concerned over odd paraphernalia. But as to the definition of the word 'heathen' —from a strict standpoint of theology I am forced to consider any sect that does not admit authority of the Vicar on Earth—"

"Don't play with me, man! I'm in no mood for it."

"I am not playing with you, David. I was about to

add that in spite of the strict logic of theology, God in His mercy and infinite wisdom will find some way to let even one like yourself into the Holy City. Now as for these priests of Mota, I have not searched their creed for flaws, but it seems to me that they are doing useful work; work that I have not been able to accomplish."

"That is exactly what worries me, Francis. There was a woman in my congregation who was suffering from an incurable cancer. I knew of cases like hers that had apparently been helped by . . . by those charlatans! What was I to do? I prayed and found no answer."

"What did you do?"

"In a moment of weakness I sent her to them."

"Well?"

"They cured her."

"Then I wouldn't worry about it too much. God has more vessels than you and me."

"Wait a moment. She came back to my church just once. Then she went away again. She entered the sanctuary, if you can call it that, that they have set up for women. She's gone, lost entirely to those idolaters! It has tortured me, Francis. What does it avail to heal her mortal body if it jeopardizes her soul?"

"Was she a good woman?"

"One of the best."

"Then I think God will look out for her soul, without your assistance, or mine. Besides, David," he continued, refilling his pipe, "those so-called priests— They are not above seeking your help, or mine, in spiritual matters. They don't perform weddings, you know. If you should wish to use their buildings, I am sure you would find it easy—"

"I can't imagine it!"

"Perhaps, perhaps, but I found a listening device concealed in my confessional—" The priest's mouth became momentarily a thin angry line. "Since then I've been borrowing a corner of the temple to listen to anything which might possibly be of interest to our Asiatic masters."

"Francis, you haven't!" Then, more moderately, "Does your bishop know of this?"

"Well, now, the bishop is a very busy man—"

"Really, Francis—"

"Now, now—I did write him a letter, explaining the situation as clearly as possible. One of these days I will find someone who is traveling in that direction and can carry it to him. I dislike to turn church business over to a public translator; it might be garbled."

"Then you haven't told him?"

"Didn't I just say that I had written him a letter? God has seen that letter; it won't harm the bishop to wait to read it."

It was nearly two months later that David Wood was sworn into the Secret Service of the United States Army. He was only mildly surprised when he found that his old friend, Father Doyle, was able to exchange recognition signals with him.

It grew and it grew. Organization—*and* communication—underneath each gaudy temple, shielded from any possible detection by orthodox science, operators stood watch and watch, heel and toe, at the pararadio equipment operating in one band of additional spectra—operators who never saw the light of day, who never saw anyone but the priest of their own temple; men marked as missing in the fields of the Asiatic warlords; men who accepted their arduous routine philosophically as the necessary exigency of war. Their morale was high, they were free men again, free and fighting, and they looked forward to the day when their efforts would free all men, from coast to coast.

Back in the Citadel women in headphones neatly typed everything that the pararadio operators had to report; typed it, classified it, condensed it, cross-indexed it. Twice a day the communication watch officer laid a brief of the preceding twelve hours on Major Ardmore's desk. Constantly throughout the day dispatches directed to Ardmore himself poured in from a dozen and a half dioceses and piled up on his desk. In addition to these myriad sheets of flimsy paper, each requiring his personal attention, reports piled up from the laboratories, for Calhoun now had enough assistants to fill every one of those ghost-crowded rooms and he worked them sixteen hours a day.

The personnel office crowded more reports on him, temperament classifications, requests for authorization, notifications that this department or that required such and such additional personnel; would the recruiting service kindly locate them? Personnel—*there* was a headache! How many men can keep a secret? There were three major divisions of personnel, inferiors in routine jobs such as the female secretaries and clerks who were kept completely insulated from any contact with the outside world; local temple personnel in contact with the public who were told only what they needed to know and were never told that they were serving in the army, and the "priests" themselves who of necessity had to be in the know.

These latter were sworn to secrecy, commissioned in the United States army, and allowed to know the real significance of the entire set-up. But even they were not trusted with the underlying secret, the scientific principles behind the miracles they performed. They were drilled in the use of the apparatus intrusted to them, drilled with care, with meticulous care, in order that they might handle their deadly symbols of office without error. But, save for the rare sorties of the original seven, no person having knowledge of the Ledbetter effect and its corollaries ever left the Citadel.

Candidates for priesthood were sent in as pilgrims from temples everywhere to the Mother Temple near Denver. There they sojourned in the monastery, located underground on a level between the temple building and the Citadel. There they were subjected to every test of temperament that could be devised. Those who failed were sent back to their local temples to serve as lay brothers, no wiser than when they had left home.

Those who passed, those who survived tests intended to make them angry, to make them loquacious, to strain their loyalty, to crack their nerve, were interviewed by Ardmore in his *persona* as High Priest of Mota, Lord of All. Over half of them he turned down for no reason at all, hunch alone, some vague uneasiness that this was not the man.

In spite of these precautions he never once commissioned a new officer and sent him forth to preach without a deep misgiving that here perhaps was the weak link that would bring ruin to them all.

The strain was getting him. It was too much responsiblity for one man, too many details, too many decisions. He found it increasingly difficult to concentrate on the matter at hand, hard to make even simple decisions. He became uncertain of himself and correspondingly irritable. His mood infected those in contact with him and spread throughout the organization.

Something had to be done.

Ardmore was sufficiently honest with himself to recognize, if not to diagnose, his own weakness. He called Thomas into his office, and unburdened his soul. Concluding, he asked, "What do you think I should do about it, Jeff? Has the job got too big for me? Should I try to pick out somebody else to take over?"

Thomas shook his head slowly. "I don't think you ought to do that, Chief. Nobody could work any harder than you do—there are just twenty-four hours in a day. Besides, whoever relieved you would have the same problems without your intimate knowledge of the background and your imaginative grasp of what we are trying to accomplish."

"Well, I've got to do *something*. We're about to move into the second phase of this show, when we start in systematically trying to break the nerve of the PanAsians. When that reaches a crisis, we've got to have the congregation of every temple ready to act as a military unit. That means more work, not less. And I'm not ready to handle it! Good grief, man— you'd think that somebody somewhere would have worked out a science of executive organization so that a big organization could be handled without driving the man at the top crazy! For the past two hundred years the damned scientists have kept hauling gadget after gadget out of their laboratories, gadgets that simply demand big organizations to use them—but never a word about how to make those organizations run." He struck a match savagely. "It's not rational!"

"Wait a minute, Chief, wait a minute." Thomas wrinkled his brow in an intense effort to remember. "Maybe there has been such work done—I seem to recall something I read once, something about Napoleon being the last of the generals."

"Huh?"

"It's pertinent. This chap's idea was that Napoleon was the last of the great generals to exercise direct command, because the job got too big. A few years later the Germans invented the principle of staff command, and, according to this guy, generals were through—as generals. He thought that Napoleon wouldn't have stood a chance against an army headed by a general staff. Probably what you need is a staff."

"For Pete's sake, I've got a staff! A dozen secretaries and twice that many messengers and clerks—I fall over 'em."

"I don't think it was that kind of a staff he was talking about. Napoleon must have had that kind of a staff."

"Well, what did he mean?"

"I don't know exactly, but apparently it was a standard notion in modern military organization. You're not a graduate of the War College?"

"You know damn well I'm not." It was true. Thomas had guessed from very early in their association that Ardmore was a layman, improvising as he went along, and Ardmore knew that he knew; yet each had kept his mouth closed.

"Well, it seems to me that a graduate of the War College might be able to give us some hints about organization."

"Fat chance. They either died in battle, or were liquidated after the collapse. If any escaped, they are lying very low and doing their best to conceal their identity—for which you can't blame them."

"No, you can't. Well, forget it—I guess it wasn't such a good idea after all."

"Don't be hasty. It *was* a good idea. Look—armies aren't the only big organizations. Take the big corporations, like Standard Oil and U. S. Steel and General Motors—they must have worked out the same principles."

"Maybe. Some of them, anyhow—although some of them burn their executives out pretty young. Generals have to be killed with an ax, it seems to me."

"Still, some of them must know something. Will you see if you can stir out a few?"

Fifteen minutes later a punched-card selector was rapidly riffling through the personnel files of every man and woman who had been reported on by the organization. It turned out that several men of business executive experience were actually then working in the Citadel in jobs of greater or lesser administrative importance. Those were called in, and dispatches were sent out summoning about a dozen more to "make a pilgrimage" to the Mother Temple.

The first trouble shooter turned out sour. He was a high-pressure man, who had run his own business much along the lines of personal supervision which Ardmore had been using up to then. His suggestions had to do with routing and forms and personal labor savers rather than any basic change in principles. But in time several placid unhurried men were located who knew instinctively and through practice the principle of doctrinal administration.

One of them, fomerly general manager of the communications trust, was actually a student and an admirer of modern military organizational methods. Ardmore made him Chief of Staff. With his help, Ardmore selected several others: the former personnel manager of Sears, Roebuck; a man who had been permanent undersecretary of the department of public works in one of the Eastern states; executive secretary of an insurance company. Others were added as the method was developed.

It worked. Ardmore had a little trouble getting used to it at first; he had been a one-man show all his life and it was disconcerting to find himself split up into several alter egos, each one speaking with his authority, and signing his name "by direction." But in time he realized that these men actually were able to apply his own policy to a situation and arrive at a decision that he might have made himself. Those who could not he got rid of, at the suggestion of his Chief of Staff. But it was strange to be having time enough to watch other men doing HIS work HIS way under the simple but powerful scientific principle of general staff command.

He was free at last to give his attention to perfecting that policy and to deal thoroughly with the occasional really new situation which his staff referred to him for solution and development of new policy. And he slept soundly, sure that one, or more, of his "other brains" was alert and dealing with the job. He knew now that, even if he should be killed, his extended brain would continue until the task was completed.

It would be a mistake to assume that the PanAsian authorities had watched the growth and spread of the new religion with entire satisfaction, but at the critical early stage of its development they simply had not realized that they were dealing with anything dangerous. The warning of the experience of the deceased lieutenant who first made contact with the cult of Mota went unheeded, the simple facts of his tale unbelieved.

Having once established their right to travel and operate, Ardmore and Thomas impressed on each missionary the importance of being tactful and humble and of establishing friendly relations with the local authorities. The gold of the priests was very welcome to the Asiatics, involved as they were in making a depressed and recalcitrant country pay dividends, and this caused them to be more lenient with the priests of Mota than they otherwise would have been. They felt, not unreasonably, that a slave who helps to make the books balance must be a good slave. The word went around at first to encourage the priests of Mota, as they were aiding in consolidating the country.

True, some of the PanAsian police and an occasional minor official had very disconcerting experiences in dealing with priests, but, since these incidents involved loss of face to the PanAsians concerned, they were strongly disposed not to speak of them.

It took some time for enough unquestioned data to accumulate to convince the higher authorities that the priests of Mota, all of them, had several annoying—yes, even intolerable characteristics. They could not be touched. One could not even get very close to one of them—it was as if they were surrounded by a frictionless pellucid wall of glass. Vortex pistols had no effect on them. They would submit passively to arrest but somehow they never stayed in jail. Worst of all, it had become certain that a temple of Mota could not, under any circumstances, be inspected by a PanAsian.

It was not to be tolerated.

CHAPTER NINE

IT WAS NOT TOLERATED. THE PRINCE ROYAL HIMSELF ordered the arrest of Ardmore.

It was not done as crudely as that. Word was sent to the Mother Temple that the Grandson of Heaven desired the High Priest of the Lord of Mota to attend him. The message reached Ardmore in his office in the Citadel, delivered to him by his Chief of Staff, Kendig, who for the first time in their relationship showed signs of agitation. "Chief," he burst out, "a battle cruiser has landed in front of the temple, and the commanding officer says he has orders to take you along!"

Ardmore put down the papers he had been studying. "Hmm-m-m," he said, "it looks like we're getting down to the slugging. A little bit earlier than I had counted on." He frowned.

"What are you going to do about it?"

"You know my methods. What do you think I'll do about it?"

"Well—I guess you'll probably go along with him—but it worries me. I wish you wouldn't."

"What else can I do? We aren't ready yet for an open breach; a refusal would be out of character. Orderly!"

"Yes, sir!"

"Send my striker in. Tell him full robes and paraphernalia. Then present my compliments to Captain Thomas and ask him to come here at once."

"Yes, sir." The orderly was already busy with the viewphone.

Ardmore talked with Kendig and Thomas as his striker robed him. "Jeff, here's the sack—you're holding it."

"Huh?"

"If anything happens so that I lose communication with headquarters, you are commanding officer. You'll find your appointment in my desk, signed and sealed."

"But Chief—"

"Don't 'But Chief' me. I made my decision on this a long time ago. Kendig knows about it; so does the rest of the staff. I'd have had you in the staff before this if I hadn't needed you as Chief of Intelligence." Ardmore glanced in a mirror and brushed at his curly blond beard. They had all grown beards, all those who appeared in public as priests. It tended to give the comparatively hairless Asiatics a feeling of womanly inferiority while at the same time arousing a vague unallocated repugnance. "You may have noticed that no one holding a line commission has ever been made senior to you. I had this eventuality in mind."

"How about Calhoun?"

"Oh, yes—Calhoun. Your commission as a line officer automatically makes you senior to him, of course. But I'm afraid that won't cut much ice in handling him. You just have to deal with him as best you can. You've got *force majeure* at your disposal, but go easy. But I don't have to tell you that."

A messenger, dressed as an acolyte, hurried in and saluted. "Sir, the temple officer of the watch says that the PanAsian Commander is getting very impatient."

"Good. I want him to be. Are the subsonics turned on?"

"Yes, sir, they make us all very nervous."

"You can stand it; you know what it is. Tell the watch officer to have the engineer on duty vary the volume erratically with occasional complete let-ups. I want those Asiatics to be fit to be tied by the time I get there."

"Yes, sir. Any word to the cruiser commander?"

"Not directly. Have the watch officer tell him that I am at my devotions and can't be disturbed."

"Very good, sir." The messenger trotted away. *This* was something like! He would hang around where he could see the face of that skunk when he heard that one!

"I'm glad we got these new headsets fitted out in time," Ardmore observed as his striker fitted his turban to his head.

The turbans had originally been intended simply

to conceal the mechanism which produced the shining halo which floated above the heads of all priests of Mota. The turban and the halo together made a priest look about seven feet tall with consequent unfavorable effect on the psyche of the Asiatics. But Scheer had seen the possibility of concealing a short range transmitter and receiver under the turban as well; they were now standard equipment.

He settled the turban with his hands, made sure that the bone conduction receiver was firm against his mastoid, and spoke in natural low tones, apparently to no one, "Commanding officer—testing."

Apparently inside his head, a voice, muffled but distinct, answered him, "Communication watch officer—test check."

"Good," he approved. "Have direction finders crossed on me until further notice. Arrange your circuits to hook me in through the nearest temple to headquarters here. I may want Circuit A at any moment."

Circuit A was a general broadcast to every temple in the country. "Any news from Captain Downer?"

"One just this moment came in, sir; I've just sent it to your office," the inner voice informed him.

"So? Yes, I see." Ardmore stepped to his desk, flipped a switch which turned off a shining red transparency reading Priority, and tore a sheet of paper from the facsimile recorder.

"Tell the Chief," the message ran, "that something is about to bust. I can't find out what it is, but all the brasshats are looking very cocky. Watch everything and be careful." That was all, and that little possibly garbled in word of mouth relay.

178

Ardmore frowned and pursed his mouth, then signaled his orderly. "Send for Mr. Mitsui."

When Mitsui came in, Ardmore handed him the message. "I suppose you've heard that I am to be arrested?"

"It's all over the place," Mitsui acknowledged soberly, and handed the message back.

"Frank, if you were Prince Royal, what would you be trying to accomplish by arresting me?"

"Chief," protested Mitsui, distress in his eyes, "you act as if I were one of those . . . those murdering—"

"Sorry—but I still want your advice."

"Well—I guess I'd be intending to put you on ice, then clamp down on your church."

"Anything else?"

"I don't know. I don't guess I'd be doing it unless I was fairly sure that I had some way to get around your protections."

"No, I suppose so." He spoke again to the air. "Communication office, priority for Circuit A."

"Direct, or relay?"

"You send it out. I want every priest to return to his temple, if he is now out of it, and I want him to do it *fast*. Priority, urgent, acknowledge and report." He turned back to those with him.

"Now for a bite to eat, and I'll go. Our yellow friend upstairs ought to be about done to a turn by then. Anything else we should take up before I leave?"

Ardmore entered the main hall of the temple from the door in the rear of the altar. His approach to the great doors, now standing open, was a stately prog-

ress. He knew that the Asiatic commander could see
him coming; he covered the two hundred yards with
leisured dignity, attended by a throng of servers clad
in robes of red, of green, of blue, and golden. His
own vestments were immaculate white. His attendants fanned out as they neared the great archway;
he marched out and up to the fuming Asiatic alone.
"Your master wishes to see me?"

The PanAsian had difficulty in composing himself
sufficiently to speak in English. Finally he managed
to get out, "You were ordered to report to me. How
dare you—"

Ardmore cut him short. "Does your master wish to
see me?"

"Decidedly! Why didn't you—"

"Then you may escort me to him." He moved on
past the officer and marched down the steps, giving
the Asiatics the alternatives of running to catch up
with him, or trailing after. The commander of the
cruiser obeyed his first impulse to hurry, nearly fell
on the broad steps, and concluded by bringing up
ignominiously in the rear, his guard attending him.

Ardmore had been in the city chosen by the Prince
Royal as his capital before, but not since the Asiatics
had moved in. When they debarked on the munici-
pal landing platform he looked about him with concealed eagerness to see what changes had been made.
The skyways seemed to be running—probably because of the much higher percentage of Asiatic population here. Otherwise there was little apparent
change. The dome of the State capitol was visible
away to the right; he knew it to be the palace of the

warlord. They had done something to its exterior; he could not put his finger on the change but it no longer looked like Western architecture.

He was too busy for the next few minutes to look at the city. His guard, now caught up with him and surrounding him, marched him to the escalator and down into the burrows of the city. They passed through many doors, each with its guard of soldiers. Each guard presented arms to Ardmore's captor as the party passed. Ardmore solemnly returned each salute with a gesture of benediction, acting as if the salute had been intended for him and him alone. His custodian was indignant but helpless; it soon developed into a race to see which could acknowledge a salute first. The commander won, but at the cost of saluting his startled juniors first.

Ardmore took advantage of a long unbroken passageway to check his communications. "Great Lord Mota," he said, "dost thou hear thy servant?" The commander glanced at him, but said nothing.

The muffled inner voice answered at once, "Got you, Chief. You are hooked in through the temple in the capitol." It was Thomas' voice.

"The Lord Mota speaks, the servant hears. Truly it is written that little pitchers have long ears—"

"You mean the monkeys can overhear you?"

"Yea, verily, now and forever. The Lord Mota will understand igpay atinlay?"

"Sure, Chief—pig latin. Take it slow if you can."

"At-thay is oodgay. Ore-may aterlay." Satisfied, he desisted. Perhaps the PanAsians had a mike and a recorder on him even now. He hoped so, for he thought it would give them a useless headache. A man has to grow up in a language to be able to understand it scrambled.

The Prince Royal had been impelled by curiosity as much as by concern when he ordered the apprehension of the High Priest of Mota. It was true that affairs were not entirely to his liking, but he felt that his advisers were hysterical old women. When had a slave religion proved anything but an aid to the conqueror? Slaves needed a wailing wall; they went into their temples, prayed to their gods to deliver them from oppression, and came out to work in the fields and factories, relaxed and made harmless by the emotional catharsis of prayer.

"But," one of his advisers had pointed out, "it is always assumed that the gods do nothing to answer those prayers."

That was true; no one expected a god to climb down off his pedestal and actually perform. "What, if anything, has this god Mota done? Has anyone seen him?"

"No, Serene One, but—"

"Then what has he done?"

"It is difficult to say. It is impossible to enter their temples—"

"Did I not give orders not to disturb the slaves in their worship?" The Prince's tones were perilously sweet.

"True. Serene One, true," he was hastily assured, "nor have they been, but your secret police have been totally unable to enter in order to check up for you, no matter how cleverly they were disguised."

"So? Perhaps they were clumsy. What stopped them?"

The adviser shook his head. "That is the point, Serene One. None can remember what happened."

"What is that you say?—but that is ridiculous. Fetch me one to question."

The adviser spread his hands. "I regret, sire—"

"So? Of course, of course—peace be to their spirits." He smoothed an embroidered silken panel that streamed down his chest. While he thought, his eye was caught by ornately and amusingly carved chessmen set up on a table at his elbow. Idly he tried a pawn in a different square. No, that was not the solution; white to move and checkmate in four moves—that took five. He turned back. "It might be well to tax them."

"We have already tried—"

"Without my permission?" The Prince's voice was gentler than before. Sweat showed on the face of the other.

"If it were an error, Serene One, we wished the error to be ours."

"You think me capable of error?" The Prince was the author of the standard text on the administration of subject races, written while a young provincial governor in India. "Very well, we will pass it. You taxed them, heavily I presume—what then?"

"They paid it, sire."

"Triple it."

"I am sure they would pay it, for—"

"Make it tenfold. Set it so high they can *not* pay it."

"But Serene One, that is the point. The gold with

which they pay is chemically pure. Our doctors of temporal wisdom tell us that this gold is made, transmuted. There is no limit to the tax they can pay. In fact," he went on hurriedly, "it is our opinion, subject always to the correction of superior wisdom"—he bowed quickly—"that this is not a religion at all, but scientific forces of an unknown sort!"

"You are suggesting that these barbarians have greater scientific attainments than the Chosen Race?"

"Please, sire, they have *something*, and that something is demoralizing your people. The incidence of honorable suicide has climbed to an alarming high, and there have been far too many petitions to return to the land of our fathers.

"No doubt you have found means to discourage such requests?"

"Yes, Serene One, but it has only resulted in a greater number of honorable suicides among those thrown in contact with the priests of Mota. I fear to say it, but such contact seems to weaken the spirit of your children."

"Hm-m-m. I think, yes, I think that I will see this High Priest of Mota."

"When will the Serene One see him?"

"That I will tell you. In the meantime, let it be said that my learned doctors, *if* they have not lived too many years and passed their usefulness, will be able to duplicate and counteract any science the barbarians may have."

"The Serene One has spoken."

The Prince Royal watched with great interest as Ardmore approached him. The man walked without fear. And, the Prince was forced to admit, the man had a certain dignity about him, for a barbarian. This would be interesting. What was that shining thing around his head?—an amusing conceit, that.

Ardmore stopped before him and pronounced a benediction, hand raised high. Then—"You asked that I visit you, Master."

"So I did." Was the man unaware that he should kneel?

Ardmore glanced around. "Will the Master cause his servants to fetch me a chair?"

Really, the man was delightful—regrettable that he must die. Or would it be possible to keep him around the palace for diversion? Of course, that would entail the deaths of all who had watched this scene— and perhaps more such expedient deaths later, if his delicious vagaries continued. The Prince concluded that it was not the initial cost, but the upkeep.

He raised a hand. Two scandalized menials hastened up with a stool. Ardmore sat down. His eye rested on the chess table by the Prince. The Prince followed his glance and inquired, "Do you play the Battle Game?"

"A little, Master."

"How would you solve this problem?"

Ardmore got up and stood over the board. He studied it for a few moments, while the Oriental watched him. The courtiers were as silent as the pieces on the board—waiting.

"I would move this pawn—so," Ardmore announced at last.

"In such a fashion? That is a most unorthodox move."

185

"But necessary. From there it is mate in three moves—but, of course, the Master sees that."

"Of course. Yes, of course. But I did not fetch you here for chess," he added, turning away. "We must speak of other matters. I learn with sorrow that there have been complaints about your followers."

"The Master's sorrow is my sorrow. May the servant ask in what manner his children have erred?"

But the Prince was again studying the chessboard. He raised a finger; a servant was kneeling beside him with writing board. He dipped a brush in ink and quickly executed a group of ideographs, sealing the letter with his ring. The servant bowed himself away, while a messenger sped out with the dispatch.

"What was that? Oh, yes—it is reported that they lack in grace. Their manner is unseemly in dealing with the Chosen Ones."

"Will the Master help an humble priest by telling him which of his children have been guilty of lapses from propriety and in what respects that he may correct them?"

This request, the Prince admitted to himself, was awkward. In some manner this uncouth creature had managed to put him on the defensive. He was not used to being asked for details; it was improper. Furthermore there was no answer; the conduct of the priests of Mota had been impeccable, flawless, in every fashion that could be cited.

Yet his court stood there, waiting, to hear what answer he would make to this crude indecency. How went the ancient lines? " . . . Kung F'tze confounded by the question of a dolt!"

"It is not meet that the servant should question

the master. At this moment you err in the fashion of your followers."

"Your pardon, Master. Though the slave may not question, is it not written that he may pray for mercy and help? We are simple servants, possessing not the wisdom of the Sun and of the Moon. Are you not our father and our mother? Will you not, from your heights, instruct us?"

The Prince refrained from biting his lip. How had this happened? By some twist of words this barbarian had put him in the wrong again. It was not safe to let the man open his mouth! Still—this must be met; when a slave cries for mercy, honor requires an answer.

"We consent to instruct you in one particular; learn the lesson well and other aspects of wisdom will come to you of themselves." He paused and considered his words. "The manner of address used by you and your lesser priests in greeting the Chosen Ones is not seemly. This affront corrupts the character of all who see it."

"Am I to believe that the Chosen Race disdains the blessing of the Lord Mota?"

He had twisted it again! Sound policy required that the ruler assume that the gods of the slaves were authentic. "The blessing is not refused, but the form of greeting must be that of servant to master."

Ardmore was suddenly aware that he was being called with urgency. Ringing in his head was the voice of Thomas: "Chief! Chief! Can you hear me? There's a squad of police at every temple, demanding the surrender of the priests—we're getting reports in from all over the country!"

"The Lord Mota hears!" It was addressed to the Prince; would Jeff understand also?

Jeff again—"Was that to me, Chief?"

"See to it that his followers understand." The Prince had answered too quickly for Ardmore to devise another double meaning in which to speak to Thomas. But he knew something that the Prince did not know he knew. Now to use it—

"How can I instruct my priests when you are even now arresting them?" Ardmore's manner changed suddenly from humble to accusatory.

The face of the Prince was impassive, his eyes alone gave away his astonishment. Had the man guessed the nature of that dispatch? "You speak wildly."

"I do not! Even while you have been instructing me in the way that I must instruct my priests, your soldiers have been knocking at the gates of all the temples of Mota. Wait! I have a message to you from the Lord Mota: His priests do not fear worldly power. You have not succeeded in arresting them, nor would you, did not the Lord Mota bid them to surrender. In thirty minutes, after the priests have cleansed themselves spiritually *and girded themselves for the ordeal,* each will surrender himself at the threshold of his temple. Until then, woe to the soldier who attempts to violate the House of Mota!"

" 'At's telling 'em Chief! 'At's telling 'em! You mean for each temple priest to hold off thirty more minutes, then surrender—is that right? And for them to be loaded for bear, power units, communicators, and all the latest gadgets. Acknowledge, if you can."

"In the groove, Jeff." He had to chance it—four meaningless syllables to the Prince, but Jeff would understand.

"O.K., Chief. I don't know what you're up to, but we'll go along a thousand percent!"

The face of the Prince was a frozen mask. "Take him away."

For some minutes after Ardmore was gone the Serene One sat staring at the chessboard and pulling at his underlip.

They placed Ardmore in a room underground, a room with metal walls and massive locks on the door. Not content with that, he was hardly inside when he heard a soft hissing noise and saw a point at the edge of the door turn cherry red. Welding! They evidently intended to make sure that no possible human weakness of his guards could result in escape. He called the Citadel.

"Lord Mota, hear thy servant!"

"Yes, Chief."

"A wink is as good as a nod."

"Got you, Chief. You are still where you can be overheard. Slang it up. I'll get your drift!"

"The headman witch doctor hankers to chew the rag with the rest of the sky pilots."

"You want Circuit A?"

"Most bodaciously."

There was a brief pause, then Thomas answered. "O.K., Chief, you've got it. I'll stay cut in to interpret—it probably won't be necessary, since the boys have practiced this kind of double talk. Go ahead—you've got five minutes, if they are to surrender on time."

Any cipher can be broken, any code can be compromised. But the most exact academic knowledge of a language gives no clue to its slang, its colloquial allusions, its half statements, over statements, and inverted meanings. Ardmore felt logically certain that the PanAsians had planted a microphone in his cell. Very well, since they were bound to listen to his end of the conversation, let them be confused and baffled by it, uncertain whether he spoke in gibberish to his god, or had possibly lost his mind.

"Look, cherubs—mamma wants baby to go to the nice man. It's all hunkydory as long as baby-bunting carries his nice new rattle. Yea, verily, rattle is the watchword—you don't and they do. Deal this cold deck the way it's stacked and the chopstick laddies are stonkered and discombobulated. The stiff upper lip does it."

"Check me if I'm wrong, Chief. You want the priests to give themselves up, and to rattle the PanAsians by their apparent unconcern. You want them to carry it off the way you did, cool as a cucumber, and bold as brass. I also take it that you want them to hang on to their staffs, but not to use them unless you tell them to. Is that right?"

"Elementary, my dear Watson!"

"What happens after that?"

"No thirty."

"What's that? Oh, 'No thirty'—more to come on this story; you'll tell us later. All right, Chief—it's time!"

"Okey-dokey!"

Ardmore waited until he was reasonably certain that all the PanAsians not immediately concerned with guarding the prisoners would be asleep, or at least in their quarters. What he proposed to do would be effective fully only in the event that no one knew just what had happened. The chances were better at night.

He called Thomas by whistling a couple of bars of "Anchors Aweigh." He responded at once—he had not gone off duty, but had remained at the pararadio, giving the prisoners an occasional fight talk and playing records of martial music. "Yes, Chief?"

"The time has come to take a powder. Allee-allee out's in free!"

"Jailbreak?"

"In the manner of the proverbial Arab—the exact manner."

They had discussed this technique before; Thomas gave itemized instructions and then said, "Say when, Chief."

"When!"

He could almost see Thomas nod. "Right-oh! O.K., troops, get going!"

Ardmore stood up and stretched his cramped limbs. He walked over to one wall of his prison and stood so that the single light cast a shadow on the wall. That would be about right—there! He set the controls of his staff for maximum range in the primary Ledbetter effect, checked to see that the frequency band covered the Mongolian race, and adjusted it to stun rather than kill. Then he turned on power.

A few moments later he turned it off, and again regarded his shadow on the wall. This required an

191

entirely different setting, directional and with fine discrimination. He turned on the red ray of Dis to guide him in his work, completed his set-up, and again turned on power.

Quietly and without fuss, atoms of metal rearranged themselves and appeared as nitrogen, to mix harmlessly with the air. Where there had been a solid wall was now an opening the size and shape of a tall man dressed in priestly robes. He looked at it, and, as an after thought, he meticulously traced an ellipse over the head of the representation, an ellipse the size and shape of his halo. That done, he reset the controls of his staff to that he had used before, turned on power, and stepped through the opening. It was a close fit; he had to wriggle through sideways.

Outside it was necessary to step over the piled-up bodies of a dozen or more PanAsian soldiers. This was not the side of the welded-up entrance; he guessed that he would have found guards outside each and any of the four walls, probably floor and ceiling as well.

There were more doors to pass, more bodies to clamber over before he found himself outside. When he did, he was completely unoriented. "Jeff," he called, "where am I?"

"Just a second, Chief. You're—No, we can't get a fix on you, but you are on a line of bearing almost due south of the nearest temple. Are you still near the palace?"

"Just outside it."

"Then head north—it's about nine squares."

"Which way is north? I'm all turned around. No

wait a minute—I just located the Big Dipper, I'm all right."

"Hurry, Chief."

"I will." He set out at a quick dogtrot, kept it up for a couple of hundred yards, then dropped into a fast walk. Damn it, he thought, a man gets out of condition with all this desk work.

Ardmore encountered several Asiatic police, but they were in no condition to notice him; he had kept the primary effect turned on. There were no whites about—the curfew was strict—with the exception of a pair of startled street cleaners. It occurred to him that he should induce them to go with him to the temple, but he decided against it; they were in no more danger than a hundred fifty million others.

There was the temple!—its four walls glowing with the colors of attributes. He broke into a run and burst inside. The local priest was almost at his heels, arriving from the other direction.

He greeted the priest heartily, suddenly realizing the strain he had been under in finding how good it was to speak to a man of his own kind—a comrade. The two of them ducked around back of the altar and went down below to the control and communication room, where the pararadio operator and his opposite number were almost hysterically glad to see them. They offered him black coffee, which he accepted gratefully. Then he told the operator to cut out of Circuit A and establish direct two-way connection with headquarters with vision converted into the circuit.

Thomas appeared to be about to jump out of the

screen. "Whitey!" he yelled. It was the first time since the Collapse that anyone had called Ardmore by his nickname. He was not even aware that Thomas knew it. But he felt warmed by the slip.

"Hi, Jeff," he called to the image, "good to see you. Any reports in yet?"

"Some. They are coming in all the time."

"Shift to relay through the diocese offices; Circuit A is too clumsy. I want a quick report."

It was forthcoming. Within less than twenty minutes the last diocese had reported in. Every priest was back in his own temple. "Good," he told Thomas. "Now I want the proprietor in each temple set for counteraction, and wake all those monkeys up. They ought to be able to use a directional concentration down the line each priest returned on, and reach clear back to the local jailhouse."

"O.K., if you say so, Chief. May I ask why you don't simply let 'em wake up when the effect wears off?"

"Because," he explained, "if they simply come to before anybody finds them the effect will be much more mysterious than if they are found apparently dead. The object of the whole caper was to break the morale of the Asiatics. This increases the effect."

"Right—as usual, Chief. The word is going out."

"Fine. When that's done, have them check the shielding of their temples, turn on the fourteen-cycle note, and go to bed—all that aren't on duty. I imagine we'll have a busy day tomorrow."

"Yes, sir. Aren't you coming back here, Chief?"

Ardmore shook his head. "It's an unnecessary risk.

I can supervise just as effectively through television as I could if I were standing right beside you."

"Scheer is all set to fly over and pick you up. He could set her down right on the temple roof."

"Tell him thanks, but to forget it. Now you turn it over to the staff duty officer and get some sleep."

"Just as you say, Chief."

He had a midnight lunch with the local priest and some conversation, then let the priest show him to a stateroom down underground.

CHAPTER TEN

ARDMORE WAS AWAKENED BY THE OFF DUTY PARARADIO operator shaking him vigorously. "Major Ardmore! Major! Wake up!"

"Unnh. . . . M-m-m-m . . . . Wassa matter?"

"Wake up—the Citadel is calling you—urgently!"

"What time is it?"

"About eight. Hurry, sir!"

He was reasonably wide awake by the time he reached the phone. Thomas was there, on the other end, and started to talk as soon as he saw Ardmore. "A new development, Chief—and a bad one. The PanAsian police are rounding up every member of our congregations—systematically."

"H-m-m-m—it was an obvious next move, I guess. How far along are they?"

"I don't know. I called you when the first report

came in; they are coming in steadily now from all over the country."

"Well, I reckon we had better get busy." It was one thing for a priest, armed and protected, to risk arrest; these people were absolutely helpless.

"Chief—you remember what they did after the first uprising? This looks bad, Chief—I'm scared!"

Ardmore understood Thomas' fear; he felt it himself. But he did not permit his expression to show it.

"Take it easy, old son," he said in a gentle voice. "Nothing has happened to our people yet—and I don't think we'll let anything happen."

"But, Chief, what are you going to do about it? There aren't enough of us to stop them before they kill a lot of people."

"Not enough to do it directly, perhaps, but there is a way. You stick to collecting data and warn everybody not to go off half-cocked. I'll call you back in about fifteen minutes." He flipped the disconnect switch before Thomas could answer.

It required some thought. If he could equip each man with a staff, it would be simple. The shielding effect from a staff could theoretically protect a man against almost anything; except, perhaps, an A-bomb or the infiltration of poison gas. But the construction and repair department had been hard pushed to provide enough staffs to equip each new priest; one for each man was out of the question, since they lacked factory mass production. Anyhow, he needed them now—this morning.

A priest could extend his shield to include any given area or number of people, but in great extension the field became so tenuous that a well-thrown snowball would break through it. Nuts!

He realized suddenly that he was thinking of the problem in direct terms again, in spite of his conscious knowledge that such an approach was futile. What he wanted was psychological jiu-jitsu—some way to turn their own strength against them. Misdirection—that was the idea! Whatever it was they expected him to do, don't do it! Do something else.

But what else? When he thought he had found an answer to that question he called Thomas to the screen. "Jeff," he said at once, "give me Circuit A."

He spoke for some minutes to his priests, slowly and in detail, and emphasizing certain points. "Any questions?" he then asked, and spent several more minutes in dealing with such as they were relayed in from the diocese stations.

Ardmore and the local priest left the temple together. The priest attempted to persuade him to stay behind, but he brushed the objections aside. The priest was right; he knew in his heart that he should not take personal risks that could be avoided, but it was a luxury to be out from under Jeff Thomas' restraining influence.

"How do you plan to find out where they have taken our people?" asked the priest. He was a former real-estate operator named Ward, a man of considerable native intelligence. Ardmore liked him.

"Well, what would you do if I weren't along?"

"I don't know. I suppose I would walk into a police station and try to scare the information out of the flatface in charge."

"That's sound enough. Where is one?"

The central police station of the PanAsian police lay in the shadow of the palace, between eight and nine blocks to the south. They encountered many PanAsians en route, but were not interfered with. The Asiatics seemed dumbfounded to see two priests of Mota striding along in apparent unconcern. Even those garbed as police appeared uncertain what to do, as if their instructions had not covered the circumstance.

However, someone had phoned ahead; they were met on the steps by a nervous Asiatic officer who demanded of them, "Surrender! You are under arrest!"

They walked straight toward him. Ward lifted one hand in blessing and intoned, "Peace! Take me to my people."

"Don't you understand my language?" snapped the PanAsian, his voice becoming shrill. "You are under arrest!" His hand crept nervously toward his holster.

"Your earthly weapons avail you not," said Ardmore calmly, "in dealing with the great Lord Mota. He commands you to lead me to my people. Be warned!" He continued to advance until his personal screen pushed against the man's body.

It—the disembodied pressure of the invisible screen—was more than the PanAsian could stand. He fell back a pace, jerked his sidearm clear and fired point-blank. The vortex ring struck harmlessly against the screen, was absorbed by it.

"Lord Mota is impatient," remarked Ardmore in a mild tone. "Lead his servant, before the Lord Mota sucks the soul from your body." He shifted to another effect, never before used in dealing with the PanAsians.

The principle involved was very simple; a cylindrical tractor-pressor stasis was projected, forming in effect a tube. Ardmore let it rest over the man's face, then applied a tractor beam down the tube. The unfortunate PanAsian gasped for air where there was no air and pawed at his face. When his nose began to bleed, Ardmore let up on him. "Where are my children?" he inquired again as softly as before.

The police officer, probably in sheer reflex, tried to run. Ardmore nailed him with a pressor beam against the door and again applied momentarily the suction tube, this time to the fellow's midriff. "Where are they?"

"In the park," the man gasped, and regurgitated violently.

They turned with leisured dignity, and headed back down the steps, sweeping those who had pressed too close casually out of the way with the pressor beam.

The park surrounded the erstwhile State capitol building. They found the congregation herded into a hastily erected bull pen which was surrounded by ranks of Asiatic soldiers. On a platform nearby, technicians were installing television pick-up. It was easy to infer that another public "lesson" was to be given the serfs. Ardmore saw no evidence of the rather bulky apparatus used to produce the epileptogenetic ray; either it had not been brought up, or some other method of execution was to be used—perhaps the soldiers present were an enormous firing squad.

Momentarily he was tempted to use the staff to knock out all the soldiers present—they were standing at ease with arms stacked, and it was conceivably possible that he might be able to do so before they could harm, not Ardmore, but the helpless members of the congregation. But he decided against it; he had been right when he gave his orders to his priests— this was a game of bluff; he could not combat *all* of the soldiers that the PanAsian authorities could bring to bear, yet he must get this crowd safely inside the temple.

The massed people in the bull pen recognized Ward, and perhaps the high priest as well, at least by reputation. He could see sudden hope wipe despair from their faces—they surged expectantly. But he passed on by them with the briefest of blessing, Ward in his train, and hope gave way to doubt and bewilderment as they saw him stride up to the PanAsian commander and offer him the same blessing.

"Peace!" cried Ardmore. "I come to help you."

The PanAsian barked an order in his own tongue. Two PanAsians ran up to Ardmore and attempted to seize him. They slithered off the screen, tried again, and then stood looking to their superior officer for instructions, like a dog bewildered by an impossible command.

Ardmore ignored them and continued his progress until he stood immediately in front of the commander. "I am told that my people have sinned," he announced. "The Lord Mota will deal with them."

Without waiting for an answer, he turned his back on the perplexed official and shouted, "In the name

202

of Shaam, Lord of Peace!" and turned on the green ray from his staff.

He played it over the imprisoned congregation. Down they went, as if the ray were a strong gale striking a stand of wheat. In seconds' time, every man, woman and child lay limp on the ground, to all appearance dead. Ardmore turned back to the Pan-Asian officer and bowed low. "The servant asks this penance be accepted."

To say that the Oriental was disconcerted is to expose the inadequacy of language. He knew how to deal with opposition, but this whole-hearted cooperation left him without a plan; it was not in the rules.

Ardmore left him no time to think of a plan. "The Lord Mota is not content," he informed him, "and directs that I give you and your men presents—presents of gold!"

With that he switched on a dazzling white light and played it over the stacked arms of the soldiers to his right. Ward followed his motions, giving his attention to the left flank. The stacked small arms glowed and scintillated under the ray. Wherever it touched, the metal shone with a new luster, rich and ruddy. Gold! Raw gold!

The PanAsian common soldier was paid no better than common soldiers usually are. Their lines shifted uneasily, like race horses at the barrier. A sergeant stepped up to the weapons, examined one and held it up. He called out something in his own tongue, his voice showing high excitement.

The soldiers broke ranks.

They shouted and swarmed and danced. They fought each other for possession of the useless, precious weapons. They paid no attention to their officers; nor were their officers free of the gold fever.

Ardmore looked at Ward and nodded. "Let 'em have it!" he commanded, and turned his knockout ray on the PanAsian commander.

The Asiatic toppled over without learning what had hit him, for his agonized attention was on his demoralized command. Ward had gone to work on the staff officers.

Ardmore gave the American prisoners the counteracting effect while Ward disintegrated a large gate in the bull pen. There developed the most unexpected difficult part of the task—to persuade three hundred-odd, dazed and disorganized people to listen and to move all in one direction. But two loud voices and a fixed determination accomplished it. It was necessary to clear a path through the struggling, wealth-mad Orientals with the aid of the tractor and pressor beams. This gave Ardmore an idea; he used the beams on his own followers much as a goose girl touches up a flock of geese with her switch.

They made the nine blocks to the temple in ten minutes, moving at a dogtrot that left many gasping and protesting. But they made it, made it without interruption by major force, although both Ward and Ardmore found it necessary to knock out an occasional PanAsian en route.

Ardmore wiped sweat from his face when he finally stumbled in the temple door, sweat that was not due entirely to precipitate progress. "Ward," he asked with a sigh, "have you got a drink in the place?"

Thomas was calling him again before he had had

time to finish a cigarette. "Chief," he said, "we are beginning to get some reports in. I thought you would like to know."

"Go ahead."

"It looks successful—so far. Maybe twenty percent of the priests have reported so far through their bishops that they are back with their congregations."

"Any casualties?"

"Yes. We lost the entire congregation in Charleston, South Carolina. They were dead before the priest got there. He tore into the PanAsians with his staff at full power and killed maybe two or three times as many of the apes as they had killed of us before he beat his way to his temple and reported."

Ardmore shook his head at this. "Too bad. I'm sorry about his congregation, but I'm sorrier that he cut loose and killed a bunch of PanAsians. It tips my hand before I'm ready."

"But, Chief, you can't blame him—his *wife* was in that crowd!"

"I'm not blaming him. Anyhow, it's done—the gloves had to come off sooner or later; this just means that we will have to work a little faster. Any other trouble?"

"Not much. Several places they fought a sort of rear-guard action getting back to the temples and lost some people." Ardmore saw a messenger in the screen hand a sheaf of flimsies to Thomas. Thomas glanced at them and continued. "A bunch more reports, Chief. Want to hear 'em?"

"No. Give me a consolidated report when they are all in. Or when most of them are in, not later than an hour from now. I'm cutting off."

The consolidated report showed that over ninety-seven percent of the members of the cult of Mota had been safely gathered into the temples. Ardmore called a staff meeting and outlined his immediate plans. The meeting was, in effect, face to face, as Ardmore's place at the conference table was taken by the pick-up and the screen of the receiver. "We've had our hands forced," he told them. "As you know, we had not expected to start action of our own volition for another two weeks, perhaps three. But we have no choice now. As I see it, we have to act and act so fast that we will always have the jump on them."

He threw the situation open to general discussion; there was agreement that immediate action was necessary, but some disagreement as to methods. After listening to their several opinions Ardmore selected Disorganization Plan IV and told them to go ahead with preparations. "Remember," he cautioned, "once we start, it's too late to turn back. This thing moves fast and accelerates. How many basic weapons have been provided?"

The "basic weapon" was the simplest Ledbetter projector that had been designed. It looked very much like a pistol and was intended to be used in similar fashion. It projected a directional beam of the primary Ledbetter effect in the frequency band fatal in those of Mongolian blood and none other. It could be used by a layman after three minutes' instruction, since all that was required was to point it and press a trigger, but it was practically foolproof—the user literally could not harm a fly with it, much less a Caucasian man. But it was sudden death to Asiatics.

The problem of manufacturing and distributing quantities of weapons to be used in the deciding conflict had been difficult. The staffs used by the priests were out of the question; each was a precision instrument comparable to a fine Swiss watch. Scheer himself had laboriously fashioned by hand the most delicate parts of each staff, and, nevertheless, required the assistance of many other skilled metalsmiths and toolmakers to keep pace with the demand. It was all handwork; mass production was impossible until Americans once more controlled their own factories.

Furthermore, detailed instruction and arduous supervised practice were indispensable in order for a priest to become even moderately skillful in the use of the remarkable powers of his staff.

The basic weapon was the pragmatic answer. It was simple and rugged and contained no moving parts other than the activating switch, or trigger. Even so, it could not be manufactured in quantity at the Citadel, as there would have been no way to distribute the weapons to widely separated parts of the country without attracting unhealthy attention from the PanAsian authorities. Each priest carried to his own temple one sample of the basic weapon; it was then his responsibility to locate and enlist in his own community, workmen with the necessary skill in metalwork for producing the comparatively simple device.

In the secret places down underneath each temple, workmen had been busy for weeks at the task—

grinding, polishing, shaping, reproducing by hand row on row of the lethal little gadgets.

The supply staff officer gave Ardmore the information he had requested. "Very well," Ardmore acknowledged, "that's fewer weapons than we have members of our congregations, but it will have to do. There will be a lot of dead wood, anyway. This damned cult business has attracted every screwball and crackpot in the country—all the long-haired men and short-haired women. By the time we count them out we may have a few basic weapons left over. Which reminds me—if we do have any left over, there ought to be some women in every congregation who are young and strong and tough-minded enough to be useful in a fight. We'll arm them. About the crackpots—you'll find a note in the general indoctrination plan as to how each priest is to break the news to his flock that the whole thing is really a hoax for military purposes. I want to add to it. Nine people out of ten will be overjoyed to hear the truth and strongly cooperative. That tenth one may cause trouble, get hysterical, maybe try to do a bunk out of the temple. Caution each priest, for God's sake, to be careful; break the news to them in small numbers at a time, and be ready to turn the sleepy ray on anybody that looks like a source of trouble. Then lock 'em up until the fun is over—we haven't time to try to reorient the soft-minded.

"Now get on with it. The priests will need the rest of the day to indoctrinate their congregations and to get them organized into something resembling military lines. Thomas, I want the scout car assigned tonight to the job involving the Prince Royal to stop here first and pick me up. Have Wilkie and Scheer man it."

"Very well, sir. But I had planned to be in that car myself. Do you object to that slight change?"

"I do," Ardmore said dryly. "If you will look at Disorganization Plan IV you will see that it calls for the commanding officer to remain in the Citadel. Since I am already here, outside the Citadel, you will remain in my place."

"But, Chief—"

"We are not going to risk both of us, not at this stage of the game. Now pipe down."

"Yes, sir."

Ardmore was called back to the communicator later that morning. The face of the headquarters communication watch officer peered out of the screen at him. "Oh—Major Ardmore, Salt Lake City is trying to reach you with a priority routing."

"Put them on."

The face gave way to that of the priest at Salt Lake City.

"Chief," he began, "we've got a most extr'ordinary prisoner. I'm of the opinion you'd better question him yourself."

"I'm short of time. Why?"

"Well, he's a PanAsian, but claims he is a white man and that you will know him. The funny thing about it is that he got past our screen. I thought that was impossible."

"So it is. Let me see him."

It was Downer, as Ardmore had begun to suspect. Ardmore introduced him to the local priest and assured that official that his screens had not failed him. "Now, Captain, out with it—"

"Sir, I decided to come in and report to you in detail because things are coming to a head."

"I know it. Give me all the details you can."

"I will, sir. I wonder if you have any idea how much damage you've done the enemy already?—their morale is cracking up like rotten ice in a thaw. They are all nervous, uncertain of themselves. What happened?"

Ardmore sketched out briefly the events of the past twenty-four hours, his own arrest, the arrest of the priests, the arrest of the entire cult of Mota, and the subsequent delivery. Downer nodded. "That explains it. I couldn't really tell what had happened; they never tell a common soldier anything—but I could see them going to pieces, and I thought you had better know."

"What happened?"

"Well—I guess I had better just tell you what I saw, and let you make your own inferences. The second battalion of the Dragon Regiment at Salt Lake City is under arrest. I heard a rumor that every officer in it had committed suicide. I suppose that is the outfit that let the local congregation escape, but I don't know."

"Probably. Go ahead."

"All I know is what I saw. They were marched in about the middle of the morning with their banners reversed and confined to their barracks, with a heavy guard around the buildings. But that's not all. It affects more than the one outfit under arrest. Chief, you know how an entire regiment will go to pieces if the colonel starts losing his grip?"

"I do. Is that the way they act?"

"Yes—at least the command stationed at Salt Lake City. I'm damned well certain that the big shot there is afraid of something he can't understand, and his fear has infected his troops, right down to the ordinary soldiers. Suicides, lots of 'em, even among the common soldiers. A man will get moody for about a day, then sit down facing toward the Pacific and rip out his guts.

"But here is the tip-off, the thing that proves that morale is bad all over the country. There has been a general order issued by the Prince Royal, in the name of the Heavenly Emperor, forbidding any more honorable suicides."

"What effect did that have?"

"Too soon to tell—it just came out today. But you don't appreciate what that means, Chief. You have to live among these people, as I have, to appreciate it. With the PanAsians, everything is face—*everything*. They care more for appearances than an American can possibly understand. To tell a man who has lost face that he can't balance the books and get square with his ancestors by committing suicide is to take the heart right out of him. It jeopardizes his most precious possession.

"You can count on it that the Prince Royal is scared, too, or he would never have resorted to any such measures. He must have lost an incredible number of his officers lately ever to have thought of such a thing."

"That is reassuring. Before this night is out, I

think we will have damaged their morale at least as much more as we have already. So you think we've got them on the run?"

"I didn't say that, Major—don't ever think so. These damned yellow baboons"—he spoke quite earnestly, evidently forgetting his own exact physical resemblance to the Asiatics—"are just about four times as deadly and dangerous in their present frames of mind as they were when they were cock o' the walk. They are likely to run amuck with just a slight push and start slaughtering right and left—babies, women—indiscriminately!"

"H-m-m. Any recommendations?"

"Yes, Chief, I have. Hit 'em with everything you've got just as soon as possible, and before they start in on a general massacre. You've got 'em softened up now—sock it to 'em!—before they have time to think about the general population. Otherwise you'll have a blood letting that will make the Collapse look like a tea party.

"That's the other reason I came in," he added. "I didn't want to find myself ordered out to butcher my own kind."

Downer's report left Ardmore plenty to wory about. He conceded that Downer was probably right in his judgment of the workings of the Oriental mind. The thing that Downer warned against—retaliation against the civilian population—always had been the key to the whole problem—that was why the religion of Mota had been founded; because they dare not strike directly for fear of systematic retaliation against the helpless. Now—if Downer was a judge—in attacking indirectly, Ardmore had rendered an hysterical retaliation almost as probable.

Should he call off Plan IV and attack today?

No—it simply was not practicable. The priests had to have a few hours at least in which to organize the men of their flocks into guerrilla warriors. That being the case, one might as well go ahead with Plan IV and soften up the war lords still further. Once it was under way, the PanAsians would be much too busy to plan massacres.

A small, neat scout car dropped from a great height and settled softly and noiselessly on the roof of the temple in the capital city of the Prince Royal. Ardmore stepped up to it as the wide door in its side opened and Wilkie climbed out. He saluted. "Howdy, Chief!"

"H'lo, Bob. Right on time, I see—just midnight. Think you were spotted?"

"I don't think so; at least, no one turned a spot on us. And we cruised high and fast; this gravitic control is great stuff." As they climbed in, Scheer gave his C.O. a brief nod accompanied by, "Evening, sir," with his hands still on the controls. As soon as the safety belts were buckled he shot the car vertically into the air.

"Orders, sir?"

"Roof of the palace—and be careful."

Without lights, at great speed, with no power source the enemy could detect, the little car plummeted to the roof designated. Wilkie started to open the door. Ardmore checked him. "Look around first."

An Asiatic cruiser, on routine patrol over the residence of the vice-royal, changed course and stabbed out with a searchlight. The radar-guided beam settled on the scout car.

"Can you hit him at this range?" inquired Ardmore, whispering unnecessarily.

"Easiest thing in the world, Chief." Cross hairs matched on the target; Wilkie depressed his thumb. Nothing seemed to happen, but the beam of the searchlight swept on past them.

"Are you sure you hit him?" Ardmore inquired doubtfully.

"Certain. That ship'll go ahead on automatic control till her fuel gives out. But it's a dead hand at the helm."

"O.K., Scheer, you take Wilkie's place at the projector. Don't let fly unless you are spotted. If we aren't back in thirty minutes, return to the Citadel. Come on, Wilkie—now for a little hocus-pocus."

Scheer acknowledged the order, but it was evident from the way his powerful jaw muscles worked that he did not like it. Ardmore and Wilkie, each attired in the full regalia of a priest, moved out across the roof in search of a way down. Ardmore kept his staff set and projecting in the wave band to which Mongolians were sensitive, but at a power-level anesthetic rather than lethal in its effect. The entire palace had been radiated with a cone of these frequencies before they had landed, using the much more powerful projector mounted in the scout car. Presumably every Asiatic in the building was unconscious—Ardmore was not taking unnecessary chances.

They found an access door to the roof, which saved them cutting a hole, and crept down a steep iron stairway intended only for janitors and repair men. Once inside, Ardmore had trouble orienting himself and feared that he would be forced to find a PanAsian, resuscitate him, and wring the location of the Prince's private chambers out of him by most ungentle methods. But luck favored them; he happened on the right floor and correctly inferred the portal of the Prince's apartment by the size and nature of the guard collapsed outside of it.

The door was not locked; the Prince depended on a military watch being kept rather than keys and bolts—he had never turned a key in his life. They found him lying in his bed, a book fallen from his limp fingers. A personal attendant lay crumpled in each of the four corners of the spacious room.

Wilkie eyed the Prince with interest. "So that's his nibs. What do we do now, Major?"

"You get on one side of the bed; I'll get on the other. I want him to be forced to divide his attention two ways. And stand up close so that he will have to look up at you. I'll talk all the business, but you throw in a remark or two every now and then to force him to split his attention."

"What sort of a remark?"

"Just priestly mumbo-jumbo. Impressive and no real meaning. Can you do it?"

"I think so—I used to sell magazine subscriptions."

"O.K. This guy is a tough nut—really tough. I am going to try to get at him with the two basic congenital fears common to everybody; fear of constriction and fear of falling. I could handle it with my staff but it will be simpler if you do it with yours. Do you think you can follow my motions and catch what I want done?"

"Can you make it a little clearer than that?"

Ardmore explained in detail, then added, "All right—let's get busy. Take your place." He turned on the four colored lights of his staff. Wilkie did likewise. Ardmore stepped across the room and switched out the lights of the room.

When the PanAsian Prince Royal, Grandson of the Heavenly One and ruler in his name of the Imperial Western Realm, came to his senses, he saw standing over him in the darkness two impressive figures. The taller was garbed in robes of shimmering, milky luminescence. His turban, too, glowed with a soft white fire—a halo.

The staff in his left hand streamed light from all four faces of its cubical capital—ruby, golden, emerald, and sapphire.

The second figure was like the first, save that his robes glowed ruddy like iron on an anvil. The face of each was partially illuminated by the rays from their wands.

The figure in shining white raised his right hand in a gesture not benign, but imperious. "We meet again, O unhappy Prince!"

The Prince had been trained truly and well; fear was not natural to him. He started to sit up, but an impalpable force shoved against his chest and thrust him back against the bed. He started to speak.

The air was sucked from his throat. "Be silent, child of iniquity! The Lord Mota speaks through me. You will listen in peace."

Wilkie judged it to be about time to divert the Asiatic's attention. He intoned, "Great is the Lord Mota!"

Ardmore continued, "Your hands are wet with the blood of innocence. There must be an end to it!"

"Just is the Lord Mota!"

"You have oppressed his people. You have left the land of your fathers, bringing with you fire and sword. You must return!"

"Patient is the Lord Mota!"

"But you have tried his patience," agreed Ardmore. "Now he is angry with you. I bring you warning; see that you heed it!"

"Merciful is the Lord Mota!"

"Go back to the place whence you came—go back at once, taking with you all your people—and return not again!" Ardmore thrust out a hand and closed it slowly. "Heed not this warning—the breath will be crushed from your body!" The pressure across the chest of the Oriental increased intolerably, his eyes bulged out, he gasped for air.

"Heed not this warning—you will be cast down from your high place!" The Prince felt himself suddenly become light; he was cast into the air, pressed hard against the high ceiling. Just as suddenly his support left him; he fell heavily back to the bed.

"So speaks my Lord Mota!"

"Wise is the man who heeds him!" Wilkie was running short of choruses.

Ardmore was ready to conclude. His eye swept around the room and noted something he had seen before—the Prince's ubiquitous chess table. It was set up by the head of the bed, as if the Prince amused himself with it on sleepless nights. Apparently the man set much store by the game. Ardmore added a postscript. "My Lord Mota is done—but heed the advice of an old man: men and women are *not* pieces in a game!" An invisible hand swept the costly, beautiful chessmen to the floor. In spite of his rough handling, the Prince had sufficient spirit left in him to glare.

"And now my Lord Shaam bids you sleep." The green light flared up to greater brilliance; the Prince went limp.

"Whew!" sighed Ardmore. "I'm glad that's over. Nice cooperation, Wilkie—I was never cut out to be an actor." He hoisted up one side of his robes and dug a package of cigarettes out of his pants pocket. "Better have one," he offered. "We've got a really dirty job ahead of us."

"Thanks," said Wilkie, accepting the offer. "Look, Chief—is it really necessary to kill everybody here? I don't relish it."

"Don't get chicken, son," admonished Ardmore with an edge in his voice. "This is war—and war is no joke. There is no such thing as humane war. This is a military fortress we are in; it is necessary to our plans that it be reduced completely. We couldn't do it from the air because the plan requires keeping the Prince alive."

"Why wouldn't it do just as well to leave them unconscious?"

"You argue too much. Part of the disorganization plan is to leave the Prince still alive and in command, but cut off from all his usual assistants. That will create a turmoil of inefficiency much greater

218

than if we had simply killed him and let their command devolve to their number-two man. You know that. Get on with your job."

With the lethal ray from their staffs turned to maximum power, they swept the walls and floor and ceiling, carying death to Asiatics for hundreds of feet—through rock and metal, plaster and wood. Wilkie did his job with white-lipped efficiency.

Five minutes later they were carving the stratosphere for home—the Citadel.

Eleven other scout cars were hurrying through the night. In Cincinnati, in Chicago, in Dallas, in major cities across the breadth of the continent they dove out of the darkness, silencing opposition where they found it, and landed little squads of intent and resolute men. In they went, past sleeping guards, and dragged out local senior officials of the PanAsians—provincial governors, military commanders, the men on horseback. They dumped each unconscious kidnaped Oriental on the roof of the local temple of Mota, there to be received and dragged down below by the arms of a robed and bearded priest.

Then to the next city to repeat it again, as long as the night lasted.

CHAPTER ELEVEN

CALHOUN BUTTONHOLED ARDMORE ALMOST AS SOON as he was back in the Citadel. "Major Ardmore," he announced, clearing his throat, "I have waited up to discuss a matter of import with you."

This man, Ardmore thought, can pick the damnedest times for a conference. "Yes?"

"I believe you expect a rapid culmination of events?"

"Things are coming to a head, yes."

"I presume the issue will be decided very presently. I have not been able to get the details I want from your man Thomas—he is not very cooperative; I fail to see why you have thrust him up to the position of speaking for you in your absence—but that is beside the point," Calhoun conceded with a magnanimous gesture. "What I wanted to say is this: Have you given any thought to the form of government after we drive out the Asiatic invader?"

What the devil was the man getting at? "Not particularly—why should I? Of course, there will have to be a sort of provisional interim period, military government of sorts, while we locate all the old officials left alive and get them back on the job and arrange for a national election. But that ought not to be too hard—we'll have the local priests to work through."

Calhoun's eyebrows shot up. "Do you really mean to tell me, my dear man, that you are seriously contemplating returning to the outmoded inefficiencies of elections and all that sort of thing?"

Ardmore stared at him. "What else are you suggesting?"

"It seems obvious. We have here a unique opportunity to break with the stupidities of the past and substitute a truly scientific rule, headed by a man chosen for his intelligence and scientific training rather than for his skill in catering to the prejudices of the mob."

"Dictatorship, eh? And where would I find such a man?" Ardmore's voice was disarmingly, dangerously gentle.

Calhoun did not speak, but indicated by the slightest of smug self-deprecatory gestures that Ardmore would not have far to look to find the right man.

Ardmore chose not to notice Calhoun's implied willingness to serve. "Never mind," he said, and his voice was no longer gentle, but sharp. "Colonel Calhoun, I dislike to have to remind you of your duty—but understand this: you and I are military men. It is not the business of military men to monkey with politics. You and I hold our commissions by grace of a constitution, and our sole duty is to that constitution. If the people of the United States want to streamline their government, they will let us know!

"In the meantime, you have military duties, and so do I. Go ahead with yours."

Calhoun seemed about to burst into speech. Ardmore cut him short. "That is all. Carry out your orders, sir!"

Calhoun turned abruptly and left.

Ardmore called his Chief of Intelligence to him. "Thomas," he said, "I want a close, but discreet, check kept on Colonel Calhoun's movements."

"Yes, sir."

"The last of the scout cars are in, sir."

"Good. How does the tally stand now?" Ardmore asked.

"Just a moment, sir. It was running about six raids to a ship—with this last one that makes a total of . . . uh . . . nine and two makes eleven—seventy-one prisoners in sixty-eight raids. Some of them doubled up."

"Any casualties?"

"Only to the PanAsians—"

"Damn it—that's what I meant! No, I mean to our men, of course."

"None, Major. One man got a broken arm when he fell down a staircase in the dark."

"I guess we can stand that. We should get some reports on the local demonstrations—at least from the East coast cities—before long. Let me know."

"I will."

"Would you mind telling my orderly to step in as

you leave? I want to send for some caffeine tablets—better have one yourself; this is going to be a big day."

"A good notion, Major." The communications aide went out.

In sixty-eight cities throughout the land, preparations were in progress for the demonstrations that constituted Phase 2 of Disorganization Plan IV. The priest of the temple in Oklahoma City had delegated part of his local task to two men, Patrick Minkowski, taxi driver, and John W. (Jack) Smyth, retail merchant. They were engaged in fitting leg irons to the ankles of the Voice of the Hand, PanAsian administrator of Oklahoma City. The limp, naked body of the Oriental lay on a long table in a workshop down under the temple.

"There," announced Minkowski, "that's the best job of riveting I can do without heating tools. It'll take him a while to get it off, anyway. Where's that stencil?"

"By your elbow. Captain Isaacs said he'd weld those joints with his staff after we finished; I wouldn't wory about them. Say, it seems odd to call the priest Captain Isaacs, doesn't it? Do you think we're really in the army—legally, I mean?"

"I wouldn't know about that—and as long as it gives me a chance to take a crack at those flat-faced apes, I don't care. I suppose we are, though—if you admit that Isaacs is an army officer, I guess he can take recruits. Look—do we put this stencil on his back or on his stomach?"

"I'd say to put it on both sides. It does seem

funny, though, about this army business, I mean. One day you're going to church; the next you're told it's a military outfit, and they swear you in."

"Personally, I like it," commented Minkowski. "Sergeant Minkowski—it sounds good. They wouldn't take me before on account o' my heart. As for the church part, I never took any stock in this great God Mota business, anyhow; I came for the free food and the chance to breathe in peace." He removed the stencil from the back of the Asiatic; Smyth commenced filling in the traced design of an ideograph with quick-drying indelible paint. "I wonder what that heathen writing means?"

"Didn't you hear?" asked Smyth, and told him.

A delighted grin came over Minkowski's face. "Well, I'll be damned," he said. "If anybody called me that, it wouldn't do him no good to smile when he said it. You wouldn't kid me?"

"No, indeed. I was in the communications office when they were getting the design from the Mother Temple—I mean general headquarters. Here's another funny thing, too. I saw the chap in the screen who was passing out the design, and he was Asiatic as this monkey"—Smyth indicated the unconscious Voice of the Hand—"but they called him Captain Downer and treated him like one of us. What do you make of that?"

"Couldn't say. He must be on our side, or else he wouldn't be loose in headquarters. What'll we do with the rest of the paint?"

Between them they found something to do with it, which Captain Isaacs noticed at once when he came in to see how they were progressing. He suppressed a smile. "I see you have elaborated on your instructions a bit," he commented, trying to keep his voice soberly official.

"It seemed a pity to waste the paint," Minkowski explained ingenuously. "Besides, he looked so naked the way he was."

"That's a matter of opinion. Personally, I would say that he looks nakeder now. We'll drop the point; hurry up and get his head shaved. I want to leave any time now."

Minkowski and Smyth waited at the door of the temple five minutes later, the Voice of the Hand rolled in a blanket on the floor between them. They saw a sleek duocycle station wagon come shooting up to the curb in front of the temple and brake to a sudden stop. Its bell sounded, and Captain Isaacs' face appeared in the window of the driver's compartment. Minkowski threw down the butt of a cigarette and grabbed the shoulders of the muffled figure at their feet; Smyth took the legs and they trotted clumsily and heavily out to the car.

"Dump him in the back," ordered Captain Isaacs.

That done, Minkowski took the wheel while Isaacs and Smyth crouched in the back with the subject of the pending demonstration.

"I want you to find a considerable gathering of PanAsians almost anywhere," directed the captain. "If there are Americans present, too, so much the better. Drive fast and pay no attention to anyone. I'll take care of any difficulties with my staff." He settled himself to watch the street over Minkowski's shoulder.

"Right, Captain! Say, this is a sweet little buggy,"

he added as the car shot forward. "How did you pick it up so fast?"

"I knocked out a few of our Oriental friends," answered Isaacs briefly. "Watch that signal!"

"Got it!" The car slewed around and dodged under the nose of oncoming cross traffic. A PanAsian policeman was left futilely waving at them.

A few seconds later Minkowski demanded, "How about that spot up ahead, Captain?" and hooked his chin in the indicated direction. It was the square of the civic center.

"O.K." He bent over the silent figure on the floor of the car, busy with his staff.

The Asiatic began to struggle. Smyth fell on him and pinned the blanket more firmly about the head and shoulders of their victim. "Pick your spot. When you stop, we'll be ready."

The car lurched to a stomach-twisting halt. Smyth slammed open the rear door; he and Isaacs grabbed corners of the blanket and rolled the now-conscious official into the street. "Take it away, Pat!"

The car jumped forward, leaving startled and scandalized Asiatics to deal with an utterly disgraceful situation as best they might. Twenty minutes later a brief but explicit account of their exploit was handed to Ardmore in his office at the Citadel. He glanced over it and passed it to Thomas. "Here's a crew with imagination, Jeff."

Thomas took the report and read it, then nodded agreement. "I hope they all do as well. Perhaps we should have given more detailed instructions."

"I don't think so. Detailed instructions are the death of initiative. This way we have them all striving to think up some particularly annoying way to get under the skins of our slant-eyed lords. I expect some very amusing and ingenious results."

By nine a.m., headquarters time, each one of the seventy-odd PanAsian major officials had been returned alive, but permanently, unbearably disgraced, to his racial brethren. In all cases, so far as the data at hand went, there had been no cause given to the Asiatics to associate their latest trouble directly with the cult of Mota. It was simply catastrophe, psychological catastrophe of the worst sort, which had struck in the night without warning and without trace.

"You have not set the time for Phase 3 as yet, Major," Thomas reminded Ardmore when all reports were in.

"I know it. I don't expect it to be more than two hours from now at the outside. We've got to give them a little time to appreciate what has happened to them. The force of demoralization will be many times as great when they have had time to compare notes around the country and realize that *all* of their top men have been publicly humiliated. That, combined with the fact that we crippled their continental headquarters almost to the limit, should produce as sweet a case of mass hysteria as one could wish. But we'll have to give it time to spread. Is Downer on deck?"

"He's standing by in the communications watch office."

"Tell them to cut in a relay circuit from him to my office. I want to listen to what he picks up here."

Thomas dialed with the interoffice communicator and spoke briefly. Very shortly Downer's pseudo-Asiatic countenance showed on the screen above Ardmore's desk. Ardmore spoke to him. Downer slipped an earphone off one ear and gave him an inquiring look.

"I said, 'Are you getting anything yet?' " repeated Ardmore.

"Some. They're in quite an uproar. What I've been able to translate is being canned." He flicked a thumb toward the microphone which hung in front of his face. A preoccupied, listening look came into his eyes, and he added, "San Francisco is trying to raise the palace—"

"Don't let me interrupt you," said Ardmore, and closed his own transmitter.

"—the Emperor's Hand there is reported dead. San Francisco wants some sort of authorization— Wait a minute; the comm office wants me to try another wave length. There it comes—they're using the Prince Royal's signal, but it's in the provincial governor's frequency. I can't get what they're saying; it's either coded or in a dialect I don't know. Watch officer, try another wave band—I'm just wasting time on that one. . . . That's better." Downer's face became intent, then suddenly lit up. "Chief, get this: Somebody is saying that the Governor of the gulf province has lost his mind and asks permission to supersede him! Here's another—wants to know what's wrong with the palace circuits and how to reach the palace— wants to report an uprising—"

Ardmore cut back in. "Where?"

"Couldn't catch it. Every frequency is jammed

229

with traffic, and about half of it is incoherent. They don't give each other time to clear—send right through another message."

There was a gentle knock at the outer door of Ardmore's office. It opened a few inches and Dr. Brooks' head appeared. "May I come in?"

"Oh—certainly, Doctor. Come in. We are listening to what Captain Downer can pick up from the radio."

"Too bad we haven't a dozen of him—translators, I mean."

"Yes, but there doesn't seem to be much to pick up but a general impression." They listened to what Downer could pick up for the better part of an hour, mostly disjointed or partial messages, but it was made increasingly evident that the sabotage of the palace organization, plus the terrific emotional impact of the disgrace of key administrators, had played hob with the normal, smooth functioning of the PanAsian government. Finally Downer said, "Here's a general order going out— Wait a minute— It orders a radio silence on all clear-speech messages; everything has to be coded."

Ardmore glanced at Thomas. "I guess that is about the right point, Jeff. Somebody with horse sense and poise is trying to whip them back into shape—probably our old pal, the Prince. Time to stymie him." He rang the communications office. "O.K., Steeves," he said to the face of the watch officer, "give them power!"

"Jam 'em?"

"That's right. Warn all temples through Circuit A, and let them all do it at once."

"They are standing by now, sir. Execute?"

"Very well—execute!"

Wilkie had developed a simple little device whereby the tremendous power of the temple projectors could be rectified, if desired, to undifferentiated electromagnetic radiation in the radio frequencies—static. Now they cut loose like sunspots, electrical storms, and aurora, all hooked up together.

Downer was seen to snatch the headphones from his ears. "For the love o'— Why didn't somebody warn me?" He reapproached one receiver cautiously to an ear, and shook his head. "Dead. I'll bet we've burned out every receiver in the country."

"Maybe so," observed Ardmore to those in his office, "but we'll keep jamming them just the same." At that moment, in all the United States, there remained no general communication system but the pararadio of the cult of Mota. The Asiatic rulers could not even fall back on wired telephony; the obsolete ground lines had long since been salvaged for their copper.

"How much longer, Chief?" asked Thomas.

"Not very long. We let 'em talk long enough for them to know something hellacious is happening all over the country. Now we've cut 'em off. That should produce a feeling of panic. I want to let that panic have time to ripen and spread to every PanAsian in the country. When I figure they are ripe, we'll sock it to 'em!"

"How will you tell?"

"I can't. It will be on hunch, between ourselves.

We'll let the little darlings run around in circles for a while, not over an hour, then give 'em the works."

Dr. Brooks nervously attempted to make conversation. "It certainly will be a relief to have this entire matter settled once and for always. It's been very trying at times—" His voice trailed off.

Ardmore turned on him. "Don't ever think we can settle things 'once and for always.' "

"But surely—if we defeat the PanAsians decisively—"

"That's where you are wrong about it." The nervous strain he was under showed in his brusque manner. "We got into this jam by thinking we could settle things once and for always. We met the Asiatic threat by the Nonintercourse Act and by big West coast defenses—so they came at us over the north pole!

"We should have known better; there were plenty of lessons in history. The old French Republic tried to freeze events to one pattern with the Versailles Treaty. When that didn't work they built the Maginot Line and went to sleep behind it. What did it get them? Final blackout!

"Life is a dynamic process and can't be made static. '—and they all lived happily ever after' is fairy-tale stu—" He was interrupted by the jangling of a bell and the red flashing of the emergency transparency.

The face of the communications watch officer snapped into view on the reflectophone screen. "Major Ardmore!"

It was gone and replaced by the features of Frank

Mitsui, contorted with apprehension. "Major!" he burst out. "Colonel Calhoun—he's gone crazy!"

"Easy, man, easy! What's happened?"

"He gave me the slip—he's gone up the temple. He thinks he's the god Mota!"

CHAPTER TWELVE

ARDMORE CUT FRANK OFF BY SWITCHING TO THE COM-
munications watch officer. "Get me the control board
in the great altar—move!"

He got it, but it was not the operator on watch
that Ardmore saw. Instead it was Calhoun, bending
over the console of controls. The operator was collapsed in his chair, head lolled to the right. Ardmore
cut the connection at once and dived for the door.

Thomas and Brooks competed for second place,
leaving the orderly a hopelessly outdistanced fourth.
The three swept up the gravity chute to the temple
level at maximum acceleration, and slammed out
onto the temple floor. The altar lay before them, a
hundred feet away.

"I assigned Frank to watch him," Thomas was
trying to say when Calhoun stuck his head over the
upper rail of the altar.

"Stand fast!"

They stood. Brooks whispered, "He's got the heavy projector trained on us. Careful, Major!"

"I know it," Ardmore acknowledged, letting the words slip out of one side of his mouth. He cleared his throat. "Colonel Calhoun!"

"I am the great Lord Mota. Careful how you speak to me!"

"Yes, certainly, Lord Mota. But tell thy servant something—isn't Colonel Calhoun one of your attributes?"

Calhoun considered this. "Sometimes," he finally answered, "sometimes I think that he is. Yes, he is."

"Then I wish to speak to Colonel Calhoun." Ardmore eased forward a few steps.

"Stand still!" Calhoun crouched rigid over the projector. "My lightnings are set for white men—take care!"

"Watch it, Chief," whispered Thomas, "he can blast the whole damn place with that thing."

"Don't I know it!" Ardmore answered voicelessly, and started to resume the verbal tight-rope walk. But something had diverted Calhoun's attention. They saw him turn his head, then hastily swing the heavy projector around and depress its controls with both hands. He raised his head almost immediately, seemed to make some readjustment of the projector, and depressed the controls again. Almost simultaneously some heavy body struck him; he fell from sight behind the rail.

On the floor of the altar platform they found Calhoun struggling. But his arms were held, his legs pinioned by the limbs of a short stocky brown man—

Frank Mitsui. Frank's eyes were lifeless china, his muscles rigid.

It took four men to force Calhoun into an improvised straitjacket and to carry him down to sick bay. "As I figure it," said Thomas, watching the work party remove their psychotic burden, "Dr. Calhoun had the projector set to kill white men. The first blast didn't harm Frank, and he had to stop to reset the controls. That saved us."

"Yes—but not Frank."

"Well—you know his story. That second blast must have hit him while he was actually in the air—full power. Did you feel his arms? Coagulated instantaneously—like a hard-boiled egg."

But they had no time to dwell on the end of little Mitsui's tragic life; more minutes had passed. Ardmore and company hurried back to his office, where he found Kendig, his Chief of Staff, calmly handling the traffic of dispatches. Ardmore demanded a quick verbal résumé.

"One change, Major—they tried to A-bomb the temple in Nashville. A near miss, but it wrecked the city district south of it. Have you set the zero hour? Several dioceses have inquired."

"Not yet, but very soon. Unless you have some more data for me, I'll give them their final instructions right away on Circuit A."

"No, sir, you might as well go ahead."

When Circuit A was reported back as ready, Ardmore cleared his throat. He felt suddenly nervous. "Action in twenty minutes, gentlemen," he started in. "I want to review the main points of the plan."

He ran over it; the twelve scout cars were assigned one each to the twelve largest cities, or, rather, what was almost the same list, the twelve heaviest concentrations of PanAsian military power. The attack of the scout cars would be the signal to attack on the ground in those areas.

The scout cars, with one exception, were poised even as he spoke, in the stratosphere over their objectives.

The heavy projectors mounted in the scout cars were to inflict as much quick damage as possible on military objectives on the ground, especially barracks and air fields. Priests, being nearly invulnerable, would supplement them on the ground, as would the projectors in the temples. The "troops" made up from the congregations would harry and hunt. "Tell them when in doubt to shoot, and shoot first. Don't wait to see the whites of their eyes. The basic weapons are good for thousands of activations without recharging, and they can't possibly hurt a white man with them. Shoot anything that moves!

"Also," he added, "tell them not to be alarmed at anything strange. If it looks impossible, one of our boys is responsible; we specialize in miracles!

"That's all—good hunting!"

His last precaution referred to a special task assignment for Wilkie, Graham, Scheer, and Downer. Wilkie had been working on some special effects, with Graham's artistic collaboration. The task in battle required a team of four, but was not a part of the regular plan. Wilkie himself did not know just how well it would work, but Ardmore had assigned a scout car to them and had given them their head in the matter.

His striker had been dressing him in his robes as he spoke. He settled his turban in place, checked his personal pararadio hook-up with the communications office, and turned to say good-by to Kendig and Thomas. He noticed a queer look in Thomas' eyes, and felt his neck turn red. "You want to go, don't you, Jeff?"

Thomas did not say anything. Ardmore added, "Sure—I'm a heel. I know that. But only one of us can go to this party, and it's going to be me!"

"You've got me wrong, Chief—I don't like killing."

"So? I don't know that I do, either. Just the same I'm going out and finish Frank Mitsui's bookkeeping for him." He shook hands with both of them.

Thomas gave the signal of execution before Ardmore reached the PanAsian capital city. His pilot set him down on the roof of the temple there after the fighting in the capital had commenced, then gunned his craft away to take up his own task assignment.

Ardmore looked around. It was quiet in the immediate neighborhood of the temple; the big projector in the temple would have seen to that. He had seen one PanAsian cruiser crash while they were landing, but the speedy little scout car assigned to that task he had not been able to notice. He went down inside the temple.

It seemed deserted. A man was standing near a duocycle car parked garagelike on the temple floor. He came up and announced, "Sergeant Bryan, sir.

The priest—I mean Lieutenant Rogers—told me to wait for you."

"Very well, then—let's go." He climbed into the car. Bryan put his little fingers to his lips and whistled piercingly.

"Joe!" he shouted. A man stuck his head over the top of the altar. "Going out, Joe." The head disappeared; the great doors of the temple opened. Bryan climbed in beside Ardmore and asked, "Where to?"

"Find me the heaviest fighting—or, rather, Pan-Asians, lots of them."

"It's the same thing." The car trundled down the wide temple steps, turned right and picked up speed.

The street ran into a little circular parkway set with bushes. There were four or five figures crouched behind those bushes, and one sprawled prone on the ground. As the car slowed, Ardmore heard the sharp *ping!* of a vortex rifle or pistol—he could not tell which—and one of the crouching figures jerked and fell.

"They're in that office building," yelled Bryan in his ear.

He set his staff to radiate a narrow, thin wedge and fanned the beam up and down the building. The pinging noise stopped. An Asiatic dashed out a door that he had not yet touched and fled up the street. Ardmore cut the beam and used another setting, aiming at the figure by means of a thin bright beam of light. The light touched the man; there was a dull, heavy boom and the man disappeared. In his place was a great oily cloud which swelled and dispersed.

"Jumping Judas! What was that?" Bryan demanded.

"Colloidal explosion. I released the surface tension of his body cells. We've been saving it for this day."

"But what made him explode?"

"The pressure in his cells. They can run as high as several hundred pounds. But let's go."

The next few blocks were deserted of all but bodies; however, Ardmore kept his projector turned on and swept the buildings they passed as systematically as the speed would allow. He took advantage of the lull to call headquarters. "Any reports yet, Jeff?"

"Nothing much yet, Chief. It's too soon."

They shot out into the open before Ardmore realized where Bryan was taking him. It was the State university campus on the edge of the city, now used as barracks by the imperial army. The athletic fields and golf course adjoining had been turned into an airport.

Here for the first time he realized clearly how pitifully few were the Americans whom he had armed to destroy the PanAsians. There appeared to be a skirmish line of sorts in position off to the right: he could see the toll they were taking of the Asiatics. But there were thousands of them, enough to engulf the Americans by sheer multitude. Damn it, why hadn't the scout car assigned reduced this place? Had it met with a mishap?

He decided that the crew of the scout car had been kept busy with aircraft, too busy to clean out the barracks. He thought now that he should have fought city by city, using all available scout cars as a unit, and trusting to the jamming of the radio to permit him to do it that way. Was it too late now to

241

change? Yes—the gage was thrown, the battle was on all over the country. Now it must be fought.

He was already busy with his staff in an attempt to swing the issue. He cut into the lines of Asiatics with the primary effect set at full power, doing a satisfying amount of slaughter. Then he decided on a change in tactics—colloidal explosion. It was slower and clumsy, but the effect on morale should be advantageous.

He omitted the guide ray to make it more mysterious and sighted through a Deephole in the cube of the staff. There! One of the rats was smoke! He had them ranged now—two! Three! Four! Again and again—a dozen or more.

It was too much for the Orientals. They were brave and seasoned soldiers, but they could not fight what they did not understand. They broke and ran, back toward their barracks. Ardmore heard cheers from the scattered Americans, dominated by an authentic rebel yell. Figures rose up from cover and took out after the disorganized Asiatics.

Ardmore called headquarters again. "Circuit A!"

A few seconds' delay and he was answered, "You've got it."

"All officers, attention! Use the organic explosion as much as possible. It scares the hell out of 'em!" He repeated the message and released the circuit.

He directed Bryan to go closer to the buildings. Bryan bumped the car over a curb and complied, weaving in and out between trees. They were conscious of a terrific explosion; the car rose a few feet in the air and came lurching down on its side. Ardmore pulled himself together and attempted to get up. It was then that he realized that somehow he had held his staff clear.

The door above him was jammed. He burned his way clear with the staff and clambered out. He looked back in to Bryan. "Are you hurt?"

"Not much." Bryan shook himself. "Cracked my left collarbone, maybe."

"Here—grab my hand. Can you make it? I've got to hang on to my staff." Between them they got him out. "I'll have to leave you. Got your basic weapon?"

"Yes, sir."

"All right. Good luck." He glanced at the crater as he moved away. It was well, he thought, that he had had his shield turned on.

A few dozen Americans were moving cautiously among the buildings, shooting as they went. Twice Ardmore was fired on by men who had been told to shoot first. Good boys! Shoot anything that moves!

A PanAsian aircraft, flying low, cut slowly across the edge of the campus. It trailed a plume of heavy yellow fog. Gas! They were gassing their own troops in order to kill a handful of Americans. The bank of mist settled slowly toward the ground and rolled in his direction. He suddenly realized that this was serious, for him as well as for others. His shield was little protection against gas, for it was necessary to let air filter through it.

But he was attempting to get a line on the aircraft even as he decided that his own turn had come. The craft wavered and crashed before he could line up on it. So the scout car was on the job after all—good!

The gas came on. Could he run around the edge of it? No. Perhaps he could hold his breath and run through it, trusting to his shield for all other matters. Not likely.

Some unconscious recess of his brain gave him the answer—transmutation. A few seconds later, his staff set to radiate in a wide cone, he was blasting a hole in the deadly cloud. Back and forth he swept the cone, as if playing a stream of water with a hose, and the foggy particles changed to harmless, life-giving oxygen.

"Jeff!"

"Yes, Chief?"

"Any trouble with gas?"

"Quite a bit. In—"

"Never mind. Broadcast this on Circuit A: Set staff to—" He went on to describe how to fight that most intangible weapon.

The scout car came screaming down out of heaven, hovered, and began cruising back and forth over the dormitory barracks. The campus became suddenly very silent. That was better; apparently the pilot had just had too much to do at one time. Ardmore felt suddenly alone, the fight had moved past him while he was dealing with the gas threat. He looked around for transportation to commandeer in order to scout around and check up on the fighting in the rest of the city. The trouble with this damn battle, he thought to himself, is that it hasn't any coherence; it's every place at once. No help for it; it was in the nature of the problem.

"Chief?" It was Thomas calling.

"Go ahead, Jeff."

"Wilkie is heading your way."

"Good. Has he had any luck?"

"Yes, but just wait till you see! I caught a glimpse of it in the screen, transmitted from Kansas City. That's all now."

"O.K." He looked around again for transportation. He wanted to be around some PanAsians, some *live* PanAsians, when Wilkie arrived. There was a monocycle standing at the curb, abandoned, about a block from the campus. He appropriated it.

There were PanAsians, he discovered, in plenty near the palace—and the battle was not going too well for the Americans. He added the effort of his staff and was very busy picking out individuals and exploding them when Wilkie arrived.

Enormous, incredible, a Gargantuan manlike figure of perfect black—more than a thousand feet high, it came striding across the buildings, its feet filling the streets. It was as if the Empire State Building had gone for a stroll—a giant, three-dimensional shadow of a priest of Mota, complete with robes and staff.

It had a voice.

It had a voice that rolled with thunder, audible and distinct for miles. "Americans, arise! The day is at hand! The Disciple has come! Rise up and smite your masters!"

Ardmore wondered how the men in the car could stand the noise, wondered also if they were flying inside the projection, or somewhere above it.

The voice changed to the PanAsian tongue. Ardmore could not understand the words, but he knew the general line it would take. Downer was telling the war lords that vengeance was upon them, and that any who wished to save their yellow skins would be wise to flee at once. He was telling them that, but with a great deal more emphasis and attention to detail and with an acute knowledge of their psychological weaknesses.

The gross and horrifying pseudo-creature stopped in the park before the palace, and, leaning over, touched a massive finger to a fleeing Asiatic. The man disappeared. He straightened up and again addressed the world in PanAsian—but the square no longer contained PanAsians.

The fighting continued sporadically for hours, but it was no longer a battle; it was more in the nature of vermin extermination. Some of the Orientals surrendered; more died by their own hand; most died purposefully at the hands of their late serfs. A consolidated report from Thomas to Ardmore concerning the degree of progress in mopping up throughout the country was interrupted by the communications officer. "Urgent call from the priest in the capital city, sir."

"Put him on."

A second voice continued, "Major Ardmore?"

"Yes. Go ahead."

"We have captured the Prince Royal—"

"The hell you say!"

"Yes, sir. I request your permission to execute him."

"*No!*"

"What was that, sir?"

"No! You heard me. I'll see him at your headquarters. Mind you don't let anything happen to him!"

Ardmore took time to shave off his beard and to change into uniform before he had the Prince Royal brought before him. When at last the PanAsian ruler stood before him he looked up and said without ceremony, "Any of your people I can save will be loaded up and shipped back where they came from."

"You are gracious."

"I suppose you know by now that you were tricked, hoaxed, by science that your culture can't match. You could have wiped us out any time, almost up to the last."

The Oriental remained impassive. Ardmore hoped fervently that the calm was superficial. He continued, "What I said about your people does not apply to you. I shall hold *you* as a common criminal."

The Prince's brows shot up. "For making war?"

"No—you might argue your way out of that. For the mass murder you ordered in the territory of the United States—your 'educational' lesson. You will be tried by a jury, like any other common criminal, and, I strongly suspect—hanged by the neck until you are dead!

"That's all. Take him away."

"One moment, please."

"What is it?"

"You recall the chess problem you saw in my palace?"

"What of it?"

"Could you give me the four-move solution?"

"Oh, *that*." Ardmore laughed heartily. "You'll believe anything, won't you? I had no solution; I was simply bluffing."

It was clear for an instant that something at last had cracked the Prince's cold self-control.

He never came to trial. They found him the next morning, his head collapsed across the chess-board he had asked for.

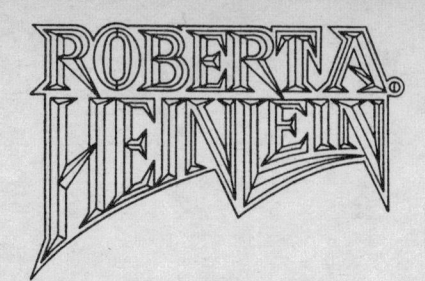

ROBERT A. HEINLEIN

"Heinlein knows more about blending provocative scientific thinking with strong human stories than any dozen other contemporary science fiction writers."
—*Chicago Sun-Times*

"Robert A. Heinlein wears imagination as though it were his private suit of clothes. What makes his work so rich is that he combines his lively, creative sense with an approach that is at once literate, informed, and exciting." —*New York Times*

Seven of Robert A. Heinlein's best-loved titles are now available in superbly packaged new Baen editions, with embossed series-look covers by artist John Melo. Collect them all by sending in the order form below:

REVOLT IN 2100, 65589-2, $3.50 ☐

METHUSELAH'S CHILDREN, 65597-3, $3.50 ☐

THE GREEN HILLS OF EARTH, 65608-2, $3.50 ☐

THE MAN WHO SOLD THE MOON, 65623-6,
$3.50 ☐

THE MENACE FROM EARTH*, 65636-8, $3.50 ☐

ASSIGNMENT IN ETERNITY**, 65637-6, $3.50 ☐

SIXTH COLUMN***, 65638-4, $3.50 ☐

---

*To be published May 1987. **To be published July 1987. ***To be published October 1987. Any books ordered prior to publication date will be shipped at no extra charge as soon as they are available.

Please send me the books I have checked above. I enclose a check or money order for the combined cover price for the titles I have ordered, plus 75 cents for first-class postage and handling (for any number of titles) made out to Baen Books, Dept. B, 260 Fifth Avenue, New York, N.Y. 10001.